For reprint permission, contact:
Tahrike Tarsile Qur'an, Inc.
80-08 51st Avenue
Elmhurst, NY 11373-4141
Tel: 718-446-6472 Fax: 718-446-4370
read@koranusa.org
www.koranusa.org

Library of Congress Cataloging-in-Publication Data: 2007923953

Barto, Linda. Where the Ghost Camel Grins.
Summary: Collection of original Muslim fables with interfaith appeal.
[1. Fables. 2. Islam, fiction. 3. Religion, fiction.]
ISBN: 978-1-879402-24-9
Printed in Canada

WHERE THE GHOST CAMEL GRINS

MUSLIM FABLES
FOR FAMILIES OF ALL FAITHS

Written and Illustrated by
Linda "iLham" Barto

Published by
Tahrike Tarsile Qur'an Inc.
© 2009

Dedicated to
my husband Thomas "TaHa" Hamsa
whose ratio of patience to blood pressure is legendary,
and to my children,
Duston the dragon warrior, and
Tana the draggin' worrier,
who have given me more adventures
than gray hairs can attest.

Special thanks
to Mrs. Nora Yount, my high school English teacher
who wouldn't stop scaring me until I learned how to write;
Dr. Muhammad Khan, who wrestled down a publisher for me;
Dr. Maqsood Jafri, who helped hold onto the publisher;
and Aun Ali Khalfan, the publisher
who finally gave in and agreed to give this book a chance.

Ultimately,
praise to Allah!

Linda "iLham" Barto

CONTENTS

Note: The Qur'an is considered to be authentic only in its original Arabic. A similar statement may be made of the Hebrew Bible. Jesus spoke Aramaic, and his words appearing in the New Testament are translations; the original Aramaic is lost. For these reasons, the words "inspired by" are used in Qur'anic and Biblical references in this book.

From the
fruit of the
date palm and
the grape vine,
you receive
wholesome drink
and food. Behold!
In this is a sign
for the wise.

inspired by
Surah 16: 67

6

Legend of the Date Seed

Islam teaches that each person is born innocent and pure. In both the Bible and Qur'an, trees are used as symbols of spiritual fruits. Good fruits of the spirit include love, generosity, patience, and honesty. Bad fruits include jealousy, selfishness, and deceit. Each person has the freedom to choose which fruits to pick –good fruits or bad fruits.

The first people that God created were Adam and Eve (peace upon them). At first, they lived in the Garden of Eden. According to the Genesis story in the Bible, there were two trees in the Garden. One tree gave the knowledge of right and wrong, and the other tree gave life (Genesis 2: 9). Some people think that the Tree of Knowledge represents disobedience and guilt. This is the tree with bad fruits for people who follow their own desires instead of God's will. The Tree of Life represents the Spirit of Wisdom, one of God's qualities. The Spirit of Wisdom helps people discover God's will in their lives.

Jewish teachers wanted to teach various concepts, so they made up parables about the Garden of Eden. One Judaic legend says that the tree that brought guilt was a handsome, grape tree. People used grapes to make wine, which leads to many sins, corruption, and poverty. For that reason, says the legend, God took away the grape tree's beauty. He made it into the spindly, twisted vine it is today. The Tree of Life, as legend has it, was a small, scraggly date tree. It helped people by giving them good dates to eat. God (blessed and exalted is He) rewarded the date palm by making it tall and beautiful.

There have been many Judaic, Christian, and Muslim legends about Adam and Eve and the Garden of Eden. The following legend has been kept secret until just the right century. Are you ready for its wisdom?

Words to know:
Allah (al-la) The Arabic word meaning <u>the God</u>, the God of Adam and Eve, Noah, Mary, Jesus, and Muhammed, and all the other prophets of God. It came from the Aramaic word 'Elah,' and Aramaic is the language Jesus spoke.
Bedouin (bed-oo-in) An Arab of any of the nomadic tribes of the deserts of North Africa, Arabia, and Syria.
Qur'an (koor-an) The Book believed by Muslims to be the <u>Revelation</u> delivered by the angel Gabriel to Prophet Muhammed (may peace be upon him!). The original Qur'an is in Arabic. A chapter is called a *surah* (soor-a).

Adam and Eve (peace upon them) had to leave the Garden of Eden. As they were leaving, Eve saw a seed on the ground under the Tree of Life. She got it and slipped it into her small pouch of woven grasses. Eve treasured the seed all her life. It was placed beside her body in a cave wherein she was laid to rest. Because the date seed was from the Garden of Eden, it never decayed but always remained fertile.

During the flood of Noah (peace upon him), the date seed was washed from the cave, and it floated out into the sea. A fish swallowed the seed. Because the seed was from the Tree of Life, the fish lived many thousands of years.

Finally, a fisherman brought up his nets heavy with many fish. Among his catch was the fish that had swallowed the date seed from the Garden of Eden. By this time, the fish had become quite huge. The fisherman was a kind and devout Jew. He sent the fish to the Holy Temple in Jerusalem to be given to the poor.

The temple priest cut the fish into portions. He gave each portion to a needy person. One portion was given to a homeless traveler. The traveler built a small fire in a bare field just outside Jerusalem. There he roasted the fish. While eating, he discovered the date seed, still inside the fish. The man simply tossed aside the date seed. The next morning, he went on to continue his journey.

When rains came to the field, the date seed sprouted. A slender, beautiful tree grew. According to the legend, this was the tree to which the Virgin Mary (peace upon her) ran for comfort.

Muslims believe in the true Gospel, and the *Qur'an records the story of Mary and Jesus. Mary received a Revelation that she would be blessed with the gift of a child. The child would be created by the very Word of *Allah. Mary was not married. When she became pregnant, her family and friends thought Mary had done something wrong. Mary became so sad that her heart felt broken. She also felt physical pain from being pregnant. The Qur'an says that "the pains of child-bearing drove her to the trunk of a palm," where she cried in distress. "But from beneath the tree, a voice spoke to her." The voice comforted Mary and told her to shake the tree. When she did, fresh, ripe dates fell for her, and a spring of water opened for her.[1] Mary gave birth to Prophet Jesus (peace upon him). He grew in the way of the Lord God (blessed and exalted is

---

[1] The story of Mary underneath the date palm is in Surah 19: 16-26.

He). The amazing story of Mary and Jesus is not based on legend. It is recorded as truth in the Qur'an.

Now the legend of the date seed continues. Jesus (peace upon him) became a young man. He saw the same date palm and ate some of its fruit. Jesus spit one of the seeds into his hand. A bird came and perched on his fingers. The bird picked up the seed and swallowed it. As the bird flew away, Jesus said, "May Allah[2] make a special blessing of you, little bird!"

The bird flew far away into Arabia. It left its droppings on the desert, and the seed was in the droppings. When rains came to the desert, the date seed was washed clean. The rainwater carried the seed to rest on a rock where it dried.

After a time, a mild, sand storm blew the seed tumbling across the desert sand. A snake saw the tumbling seed. Because the seed was moving, the snake thought it was something alive. The snake gulped the seed. Because of Jesus' blessing on the bird, this date seed was granted, by God's will, the heritage of the Garden of Eden. Because of the blessing, the snake lived for hundreds of years.

Finally, one day the snake was caught swallowing chicken eggs. His long life came to an abrupt end. A *Bedouin woman chopped off its head and threw its body out into the sun.

A hawk flying overhead spotted the headless snake writhing from nervous reflexes. The hawk fetched it, and carried it to a nest in a rocky cliff. As the snake's body was being torn apart for the hawk's supper, a morsel containing the date seed fell. The seed landed on the rocks below and was carried by a gust of wind to fertile soil. There the seed sprouted and grew into a fine, abundant palm.

Many years later, the Prophet Muhammed (peace upon him) was traveling with his companions. The food they had packed was nearly gone. They saw the palm tree in the distance. At first they thought it was a *mirage. Muhammed turned his camel toward the tree, and he was the first to reach it. As soon as Muhammed was under the tree, dates fell for him. Water bubbled up from the earth covering the tree's roots. Muhammed and his companions had enough to eat and drink.

Thus is the legend of how Jesus and Muhammed (peace and blessings upon them) were both blessed by the Tree of Life. They were truly brothers in the faith.

---

[2]Jesus would actually have used the Aramaic word *Elah* for God, which is similar to the Arabic *Allah*. Both Hebrew and Arabic evolved from Aramaic.

Do you understand how God explains by way of a parable? The good Word is like a good tree whose roots are firmly planted and whose branches extend to Heaven.

inspired by
Surah 14:24

How the Needle Got Its Eye

The Qur'an says, "Those who reject God's signs and treat them with arrogance...will not enter the Garden [of Paradise] until the camel can pass through the eye of the needle. ...." (inspired by Surah 7: 40).

In the New Testament version of the Gospel, Jesus (peace upon him) says, "It is easier for a camel to pass through the eye of a needle than it is for a rich man to enter Heaven" (inspired by Matthew 19: 24).

Some people believe that these verses refer to a rock formation called "eye of the needle." The oblong hole in the rock was narrow. A camel carrying a pack on its back could not pass through the hole. The camel's owner had to remove the camel's pack. After that, the camel could pass through easily. The moral is that a person must be willing to lay aside his or her worldly riches. He or she must focus on spiritual treasures instead of things he or she can buy with money. After doing that, he or she can come closer to God. A person must dedicate even his money to God. Very wealthy people sometimes love their money too much.

The following story is a legend of how the rock formation got its needle's eye. The hero in the story is Melchizadek (mel-ki-za-dek). The Psalms of David says that the Messiah will become "a priest like Melchizedek" (inspired by Psalms 110: 5). (The Messiah, in this verse, is the one promised by God to deliver the world from injustice.) The Torah (the first five books of the Jewish Bible) says that Melchizedek was "a priest of God Most High" (inspired by Genesis 14: 18). Melchizedek served God during the time of Abraham. He lived before the religions of Christianity and Judaism. Being "a priest like Melchizedek" means that the Messiah's help is not just for Jews. It is for all those devoted to God Most High (blessed and exalted is He). According to Hadith (the teachings of Muhammed), Jesus (peace upon him) will return to assume the authority of Messiah. Muhammed (peace upon him) said, "The son of Mary will surely come down as a fair judge."[3]

Gar had lived a very long time upon the earth. In his life he had seen people become more and more wicked. Many people abandoned God (blessed and exalted is He) and put their hopes in material things. They became greedy and worshiped idols that they believed could give them more things.

Gar believed in the One True God (blessed and exalted is He), but his faith was weak. "I cannot bear to live in this evil world any longer," Gar said to himself. "I cannot even trust my own relatives. They are always ready to steal from me. They would stab me in the back to take my land or any of my possessions."

Gar became so depressed that he decided to end his life. He chose a steep cliff from which to jump and hurled himself from the cliff's edge. The branches of a small tree broke his fall and prevented Gar's death. Even so, his body hit the ground hard. The breath was knocked out of him, and he became unconscious.

Gar's body had hit the branches so hard that the force partially uprooted the tree. From underneath the exposed roots, a spring spurted. It shot a gush of water upward. The water came down and smacked Gar in the face. He immediately gained consciousness.

Thinking that he had been dead, Gar exclaimed, "This water has the power to give life to the dead!"

The spring was bubbling into a pool now. Gar began to imagine how happy he could make everyone with this new magic.

'Perhaps,' Gar thought, 'if people were happier, they would praise *Allah and begin to do the right things.'

---

[3]A hadith reported by a follower named Muslim.

12

Gar scrambled back to his grass hut and fetched a clay bowl. He returned to the spring and filled the bowl with water. As he was returning to his village, he saw a lion's body awkwardly sprawled on a rock in the sun. Thinking the lion was dead, Gar decided to try the magic water. Gar poured the water over the lion's face, but the lion was not dead; it was only sleeping very soundly. Being abruptly awakened from his deep, peaceful sleep, the lion growled furiously and jumped toward Gar.

Gar didn't take time to ponder what a stupid idea it was to bring a fierce lion back to life. He just took off running as fast as his legs could carry him. The lion was right at Gar's heels, and Gar was screaming! Just an hour earlier, he had been ready to die, but he did not want his death to come from the terrible jaws of an angry lion.

Gar's high-pitched screams and the lion's deep roars made a lot of racket. The noise got the attention of a religious man who was meditating on a mountain side. Melchizedek (peace upon him) was a priest of God Most High (blessed and exalted is He). He often came to the wilderness to pray and seek God's guidance. When he saw that the lion was about to devour the man, Melchizedek pointed a finger at a tall, rock formation. He recited words in the direction of the rock. The words he said were the Word of God that had been given to Abraham (peace upon him): "Associate no others with Me, and purify My House for those who encompass it and for those who stand, bow, and prostrate in prayer. Proclaim to Humanity the pilgrimage. They will come to you on foot and by camel, fit and trim from traveling far on distant mountain byways. They will come to bear witness to the blessings they have and to celebrate the name of *Allah throughout the appointed days and over the livestock He has provided for them to eat and to give to the poor."[4]

The Word of God cut through the air like an arrow shot from a steady bow. It pierced the rock and broke an oblong shape out of it. The force of God's Word shattered the dislodged chunk. Pieces flew through the air. A big piece of rock hit the lion really hard on the head. The lion staggered, became confused, and forgot its pursuit.

Melchizedek (peace upon him) saw that the impending peril was solved. He calmly returned to his prayer and meditation.

---

[4]Inspired by Surah 22: 26-28. "My House" refers to the *Ka'bah* (illustrated at end of this story), a square building protecting an altar in Mecca, Saudi Arabia. Muslims believe that the altar was built by Abraham and his son Ishmael. The "pilgrimage" refers to the *hajj*, a spiritual journey Muslims make to Meccah.

Gar returned to the spring for another bowl of water, which never again brought the dead to life. Gar decided that God (blessed and exalted is He) had removed the water's magic because Gar had used it so foolishly.

Most people continued in their wickedness, but a few chose to listen to Melchizedek's preaching. Truth rather than magic brought happiness to those few. Their lives were changed. The Word of God broke the hardness of their stubborn hearts like a hammer breaks rock.

Gar was encouraged by the few who turned from their sins. He was happy about that.

The pure water was a treasure in itself, but it contained no magic. Its discovery, however, led to a special gift for Gar. Gar gained a fun-loving companion—the lion. The lion had been knocked so senseless that it reverted back to its childhood. For the rest of its life, the once-vicious lion remained an overgrown but playful kitten.

Ameera and
The Pool of Light

In pre-Islamic Arabia, people believed in fairies, elves, and wood sprites. They were called *jinn*. People believed that jinn could assume the forms of people and animals. The *Qur'an uses a different meaning for *jinn*. The jinn of the Qur'an are angelic beings (spirits) who use free will. Some do good things; some do evil things. *Iblis*, also known as Satan, was among the angels and one of the jinn, a *jinni*.

Muslims do not believe in the superstitions that preceded the truth of the Qur'an. Even so, they enjoy fairy tales just as people enjoy the tales of the brothers Grimm, Aesop's fables, and stories of leprechauns, giants, and magic beans. The following story involves a good jinni.

Before the ministry of Muhammed (peace upon him), some parents did not want their baby girls. Some parents left baby girls in the wilderness for wild animals. Some parents buried the babies alive in the hot desert sand. The Qur'an warns that those who kill babies must stand before God (blessed and exalted is He) on the Day of Judgment. They will be blamed for their actions.

Arabic words to learn:
Ameera (a-meer-a) A female name meaning <u>princess.</u>
Banat al Lah (ba-nat al la) <u>Daughters of God</u>, the pagan goddesses al Lat, al Uzza, and Manat.
Islam (i-slam) 1. Complete submission to God, the faith believed by Muslims to be the original religion ordained by God to Adam and Eve and all creation. 2. The organized religion based on the Qur'an and the *Sunnah* (examples) and *Hadith* (teachings) of Muhammed. 3. The term used by Muslims to describe the peace a believer feels when he or she submits his or her whole self to God.

*Jameela longed for a daughter, but she hoped that her new baby would be another boy. She knew that her husband *Yasir would not allow a girl to live. Daughters were considered worthless.

When the baby was born, the father saw that it was a girl. He promptly snatched her from her mother's arms. Jameela begged Yasir to let the child live, but he would not even discuss it. Jameela cried and prayed as Yasir left the house with the innocent, fragile, little girl.

16

*Wajeeh was the baby's brother. He had just returned from tending his goats. Yasir carelessly handed the naked baby to Wajeeh. "Take this shameful thing," Yasir said, "and leave it on the Pool of Light."

In the wilderness was a large rock, which had been used by ancient pagans. The top of the rock had been smoothed into a shallow, bowl-shape for blood sacrifices. It was called the Pool of Light, because its smooth surface reflected light from the sky. Under a full moon, the bowl shape looked as if it were filled with light.

"But, Father," Wajeeh argued, "if I leave the baby in the wilderness, she will starve or a wild beast may devour her."

"Do as I say!" Yasir demanded.

Wajeeh knew better than to disobey his father. Yasir's bad temper was worse than being caught in a whirlwind on the desert. Often Yasir had erupted into a violent rage. Wajeeh and his mother had suffered physical, verbal, and emotional abuse.

Wajeeh wrapped the baby in a tanned goatskin and carried her into the wilderness. It was late evening when Wajeeh laid the precious baby on the bloodstained rock. She was already crying, and he did not want to leave her.

Wajeeh knelt at the rock and prayed to the three goddesses he had been taught to worship. "Oh, *Banat al Lah, I praise you and worship you. Reward me for my worship; I beg you, al Lat, al Uzza, and Manat. Be mothers to this little child as you are mothers to me. Protect her, and send good jinn to care for her."

The goddesses were not real, but because Wajeeh's heart was right, *Allah heard his prayer. *Bushra was a kind *jinni who lived in the forest. She also heard Wajeeh's prayer. Bushra was impressed with Wajeeh's compassion and agreed to be the answer to his prayer. After Wajeeh had abandoned the infant, Bushra took the form of a mother gorilla. She cradled the baby in hairy, gorilla arms and fed her warm, sweet gorilla milk from Bushra's breast. All night Bushra protected the child and kept her warm.

In the morning, Wajeeh herded his small flock of goats to the hills to graze. He wondered about the baby, but he dreaded venturing near the Pool of Light. He was afraid the baby was dead. He did not want to find her body partially eaten by wild animals. Finally, however, he could not ignore his curiosity. He wandered toward the pagan ruins.

Bushra realized that Wajeeh was coming back. She gently laid the baby on the bowl-shaped altar and hid behind the trees.

Wajeeh was surprised and happy to see that the baby was still alive. "Praise al Banat al Lah! My goddesses watched over you during the night. You are probably starving," Wajeeh said. He scooped the baby into his arms.

Wajeeh hurried to his flock of goats and milked one of the nannies. He caught the milk in a small, tin cup that he kept with him for water. With a finger, he dropped milk into the baby's mouth.

"I will name you *Ameera*," Wajeeh said, "because you are the child of goddesses."

Wajeeh lovingly cared for *Ameera all day. When it became evening, he left her on the altar. He knew he had to keep her existence a secret, or his father would find Ameera and kill her.

Year after year, Wajeeh cared for the baby by day, and Bushra by night. Wajeeh brought clothes and food for Ameera. Wajeeh was not educated, but he taught Ameera what he knew. He showed her which plants she could eat and which were poisonous. He taught her which insects and snakes were harmful and what to do if she were bitten. He taught her how to protect herself during a storm, and how she should behave when approached by a lion or wild boar. Ameera learned to survive in the wilderness. She made friends with the birds and gentle creatures of the forest. She taught herself to make ornaments from rocks and bark. Wajeeh showed her how to make paintings with colored sand and pebbles.

Ameera was sad and lonely, however. Wajeeh was a good brother, but he could only stay with her during the day. After the goats grazed, Wajeeh took the goats and went away. Ameera could not understand why. Bushra was a good mother, and Ameera loved her, but Ameera wondered why her mother was hairy. Bushra looked so different from Wajeeh and Ameera! Ameera wondered why there was no other creature like herself. Whenever Ameera mentioned Bushra, Wajeeh thought she was just playing a pretend game. Ameera couldn't understand why. She had so many questions that Wajeeh would not answer.

When he went home in the late afternoon, Wajeeh always left Ameera at the Pool of Light. He always asked al Banat al Lah to look after her.

One day Wajeeh had turned to leave and was walking away. Ameera shouted after him, "Wajeeh, take me with you!"

Wajeeh turned around unexpectedly. Bushra had already come for Ameera. She and Wajeeh saw one another eye-to-eye. Wajeeh and Bushra both screamed—Wajeeh with fear, and Bushra with alarm at Wajeeh's discovering her.

"What's the matter with you two?" Ameera asked, confused by their reaction.

Wajeeh had never seen a gorilla. In fact, he had never even heard of a huge, hairy beast such as this. He saw that Ameera was not afraid of it. It did not appear to be a danger to her.

"What is that thing?" Wajeeh asked.

"This is my mother Bushra," Ameera told him.

Then Bushra dared speak. "I am the jinni you asked for on the first day you left Ameera on the Pool of Light."

Wajeeh gasped. "Praise al Banat al Lah!"

"Praise Allah," Bushra said, for the jinn know the truth of the One True God.

Ameera, however, was confused. "Jinni? But I thought you were my mother," she said to Bushra.

Wajeeh and Bushra were silent. They realized that it was time for the truth. Wajeeh explained to Ameera how she came to live alone in the wilderness.

Ameera said nothing. She only cried and felt as if her life had no value. She suddenly wished that she had never been born.

Wajeeh returned home very sad. When he entered the tent in which his family lived, he was surprised. His parents sat on the floor and were crying as if someone had just died.

"What has happened?" Wajeeh asked.

"Oh, Wajeeh," we committed a terrible sin, Yasir said in a broken voice.

"Sin?" Wajeeh was bewildered. "What are you talking about?"

"Your father met a traveler today," Wajeeh's mother began to explain. "He brought glad tidings for believers, but for us he brought a message of doom. He recited words to us. He said that they were words from Allah."

Yasir continued the explanation. "He said that a great prophet has received a Revelation. The Prophet of Allah recited, 'Their Sovereign Lord gives believers glad tidings of His mercy and good pleasure and of Gardens wherein are eternal delights for them. They will dwell therein forever. Verily the greatest reward is being in the presence of Allah.'"[5]

"But that is good news, Father," said Wajeeh.

Yasir began crying so hard that he could not respond.

Jameela continued, "The Prophet of Allah also said, 'When the souls are divided, and when the baby girl who was buried alive is questioned for what crime she was killed, when the scrolls are laid open, when the world on high is unveiled, when the blazing fire is kindled to fierce heat, and when the Garden is brought near, then each soul will realize what it has put forth.' This means that we will have to face Allah about the daughter born to us years ago."[6]

Yasir tried to stop crying. He said, "The Prophet of Allah said, 'That day they shall be forcibly thrust down into the fire of Hell.'"[7] Yasir wept and then said, "I have destroyed a wonderful gift from Allah—the gift of a baby girl. For this I will be eternally condemned." The sound of thunder rumbled in the distance, and it began to rain.

Wajeeh was dumbfounded. Finally, he found his voice and his nerve and said, "The girl is not dead."

Jameela and Yasir stopped crying and stared at Wajeeh in disbelief. "What?" they said in unison.

Wajeeh gulped. "I couldn't do it, Father. I couldn't just leave her there. I prayed to al Banat al Lah to protect her and to send jinn to take care of her. The goddesses did as I asked. A jinni, Bushra, a big, hairy jinni, has been a mother to her for all these years."

A streak of lightning sketched itself into the growing darkness. The rain and the rumble of thunder were the only sounds as Jameela and Yasir absorbed Wajeeh's information.

"Where is she?" Yasir finally asked.

"I left her with Bushra at the Pool of Light," Wajeeh said.

"Yasir, you must go get her," Jameela begged.

"I will! I will!" Yasir determined. "Wajeeh, stay with your mother." Yasir grabbed a cloak and headed out the door.

"Her name is Ameera," Wajeeh yelled after him.

---

[5]Inspired by Surah 9: 21-22.
[6]Inspired by Surah 81: 8-14.
[7]Inspired by Surah 52: 18.

By the time Yasir got to the hillsides, rain was pounding hard. He ran into the forest. As he neared the site of the ancient pagan rituals, a flash of lightning shared its brilliance with the Pool of Light.

"Ameera! Ameera!" Yasir called.

Ameera, safe in a cave, heard the calls and asked Bushra, "Who is that? I do not recognize that voice. That is not Wajeeh."

Bushra, being a jinni, realized what was happening. She said, "My mission is complete. It is time now for me to let you go. But remember, Ameera, I will always love you."

A terrible flash of light and the frightening crack of thunder drew Ameera's attention away. She glanced outside the cave, and then turned to Bushra for comfort. But Bushra was not there.

"Bushra?" Ameera called, but there was no answer. "Bushra?"

Ameera ran out into the rain. "Bushra, where are you?" Ameera ran farther from the cave and continued to call for Bushra in vain. The furious sounds of the storm surrounded her.

Ameera heard the strange voice calling for her. Frightened of it, she ran away from the voice. The earth had already become soft and slippery from the rain. Suddenly Ameera was tumbling down a rocky incline. She grabbed onto a bush growing down the side of a cliff. Lightning gave Ameera enough light to see. Ameera then saw that she was dangling above a ravine, now raging with muddy rapids from the torrential rains.

Yasir was soaking wet. He walked around the forest and called for Ameera, but there was no answer. Feeling helpless, he headed back toward the Pool of Light. 'Strange,' he thought as he neared the altar. Even without the flashes of lightning, the Pool of Light was glowing. He walked over to it and looked into the shimmering pool. In it, he saw a vision of his daughter hanging over the treacherous ravine. "Ameera!" he said, alarmed.

"This way," Bushra's voice called to him.

Yasir saw nothing, but he ran in the direction of the voice. He realized that Ameera was indeed in desperate trouble. Only he could save her. With the help of the flashing lightning, he found the cliff he had seen in the vision. He looked over the edge and saw

his little girl. She was holding onto a branch, but her fingers were slipping.

"Ameera," he called. "I am your father. I love you, Ameera. I am not going to hurt you." Yasir lay on a rock jutting over the cliff and reached down for Ameera. "Reach up and grab my hand. Let me help you."

Ameera had no choice but to trust him. She let one hand go of the bush and stretched her arm up as far as she could. The rain was quickly loosening the soil from the bush's roots. Just as Ameera latched onto her father's hand, the bush uprooted and fell beneath her. With both their hands slippery with rainwater, Yasir began to lose his grip on Ameera's little hand. He was afraid he was about to drop her. Just then, the rock on which Yasir was lying slid downward. The slide moved him closer to Ameera. With his other hand, he grabbed Ameera's arm and pulled her toward him. With a burst of energy, Yasir yanked Ameera upward and quickly got her and himself onto steady ground. Within an instant, the rock on which Yasir had lain came loose from the soil and crashed down the side of the cliff. It carried with it everything in its path until it plunged through empty space and crashed into the ravine below.

Yasir cried as he hugged Ameera. "Forgive me, my little child, my precious little girl. I was wrong not to love you and cherish you. Let me take you home to your mother and brother."

Ameera was restored to her family, and Bushra visited her in Ameera's dreams. The family began to learn of the One True God (blessed and exalted is He) and the commandments that He has given us to follow. Islam entered Yasir's heart and melted away his anger. Yasir found comfort when he learned that the Prophet of Allah had recited, "Allah will forgive you of your sins and grant you admittance to Gardens beneath which rivers flow and to beautiful mansions within Gardens of Eternity. That is the supreme achievement."[8]

[8]Inspired by Surah 61: 12.

Whoever rejects evil and
believes in God
has grasped the
most trustworthy
grip that never
breaks.

inspired by
Surah 2: 256

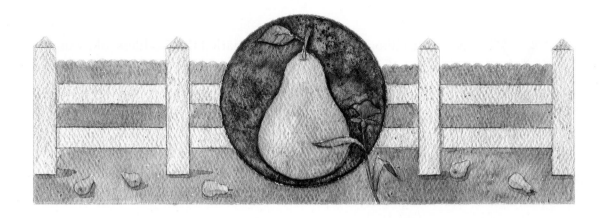

The Tree Mourns in the Rain

When Noah (peace upon him) tried to warn people that a great flood was coming, they ridiculed him. They would not believe that his Sovereign Lord had revealed anything to him. Noah's pleadings were in vain, and God said to him, "None of your people will believe except those who have already believed, so grieve no longer over their crimes" (inspired by Surah 11: 36). All people vanished forever, except those saved in the ark built by Noah.

God (blessed and exalted is He) has sent His warnings numerous times through the prophets of old. Still, many people insist on ignoring them. They live as if there is no God and no Day of Judgment. But God is always near, ready to save those who will turn to Him.

Here is a story involving a person who would not heed the warnings and would not call on God for salvation until it was too late.

Arabic words to learn:
adhan (ad-han) The Muslim call to prayer.
Al Fatiha (al fa-tee-a) <u>The Beginning</u>, the name of the first surah (chapter) of the Qur'an.
alhamdulAllah (al-ham-dul-a-la) <u>Praise God</u>.
BismAllah (bis-mal-la) <u>In the Name of God</u>.
couscous (coos-coos) A Middle Eastern pasta made of semolina and having a consistency coarser than cream of wheat and finer than grits.
imam (e-mom) Muslim prayer leader.
insh'Allah (in-sha-la) <u>If God is willing</u>.
Sunnah (soo-na) The <u>examples</u> of the Prophet Muhammed, which guide Muslims in how to live an exemplary life.
ummah (oo-ma) 1. Religious congregation of an individual church, synagogue, or mosque. 2. The universal family of Muslims. 3. The universal family of all believers of the One True God.

"Your pears are falling on my property!" snarled the toothless, old woman. The branches of Asah's tree spread slightly over the wooden slat fence erected directly on the property line.

"I will send my children to gather them," *Asah told her.

"I don't want those sniffling brats over here! You come and get them up yourself!" the woman demanded.

Asah sighed, and then gingerly hopped over the fence.

"You had better do something about this ugly tree and the messy fruit it drops into my yard," the cranky, old woman challenged. "If you don't, I'm going to sue."

Asah said nothing as she picked up the pears. She laid them on her lap while she held the two corners of her apron together with one hand. She had been living with Maisa's spiteful nature as long as Asah could remember. Asah had inherited the humble home around which her parents had planted wonderful pear, apple, and cherry trees.

"May I leave through your gate," Asah politely asked. She knew better than to assume anything.

"Hurry and be gone with you!" snapped old *Maisa. "And I don't want to see any pears on my property in the morning!"

Asah sighed and walked briskly across Maisa's yard. She opened the gate, while holding her apron together, and slipped out. She turned, and, as she closed the gate, she smiled broadly and said, "May Allah bless you really well today, Maisa."

Maisa was irritated by Asah's blessing. Maisa's eyes looked as though fire might shoot from them. "Hmmmph!" was Maisa's only response.

Maisa had nagged her husband (the unfortunate louse) to his grave, and her arrogant children had moved as far away from her as they could get. She was so nasty that even Satan avoided her; she didn't need *his* advice anyway. She was the queen of mean.

Later in the evening, Asah's husband returned from his work in the city. "What are we to do about poor Maisa?" Asah said as she peeled and cut pears for their supper. "She is so bitter and won't allow anyone to be her friend."

"Why do you even care about that old witch?" *Masoud responded.

"Well, she is one of Allah's creatures," chastised Asah.

"Yeah, but which one of the evil *jinn is she?" teased Masoud.

"Oh, Masoud! You should be ashamed talking like that. Maybe she has a good reason for acting like a rabid hyena." Asah snickered.

"Heh," Masoud chuckled. "Do hyenas get *rabies?"

"I don't know," Asah said, grinning, "but apparently toothless, old women do."

Asah and Masoud both laughed out loud.

The children bounded in. "What's funny, Mama?" *Riyad asked.

"'Wha's 'unny, Mommie?" echoed little *Azhar.

"Oh—uh—uh—oh, we were just laughing at how the pears look like funny, little people. See?" Asah quickly cut a face into a pear. She gave it to Riyad.

"Me one, Mommie! Me one," Riyad's little sister squealed with delight.

Asah cut a face into another pear for Azhar.

"Can s'eep wif it, Mommie?"

"No, you can't sleep with it; you'll get sticky all over you. But you can put it on a dish beside your bed."

"I'll show you how to dry it out," volunteered Masoud, "so you can keep it, face and all."

"Will you show me, too, Daddy?" asked Riyad.

"Right after supper," Masoud agreed. He got plates from the cabinet and set the table.

Asah set a bowl of *couscous with vegetables and a bowl of sliced pears on the table, and everyone sat down.

"You're getting to be a big boy, Riyad," Masoud said. "Would you like to say the food prayer?"

Riyad smiled and bowed his head. "O *Allah, thank You for Your grace and mercy and safekeeping. We ask that You bless the food You have provided for us, and we ask for Your salvation from the punishment of Hell. *BismAllah. Amen."

"Me p'ay too, Daddy," said Azhar.

"Okay," agreed Masoud, and everyone bowed again.

"B'ess me an' Ri'ad an' Mommie an' Daddy an' da witzh nex' door. 'A-men!'"

Masoud and Asah quickly looked up from prayer and glanced at one another. They felt a little guilty and a little humored at Azhar's reference to "the witch next door."

"Some men came in today to buy lumber for one of the villages on the other side of the hills," Masoud solemnly said as he spooned couscous into Azhar's plate. "They said that the late rains had swelled the creeks. There was a flash flood that destroyed many of their homes."

"That's strange," said Asah as she passed slices of bread. "I've lived here all my life, and we've never had that much rain."

"That's the same thing *they* said. They never suspected that the rain was building up so much," continued Masoud. "They warned everyone at work. They said that, if it begins raining again here, we should evacuate to higher ground. People in some of the lower valleys drowned, they told us."

"I've never heard of a flood that size around here," Asah insisted.

"Daddy, wha'sa fud?" asked Azhar.

Masoud stared at her while he tried to think of the right words. Finally Asah answered for him. "Honey, it's when the rain water gets so big on the ground that it knocks things over."

Azhar's eyes got big, and her mind wandered off to try to imagine such a thing.

"Where will we go, Daddy," asked Riyad.

"We can go to my folks' place up on the mountain," Masoud answered. "We'll be safe there."

In the morning, Asah got up long before dawn. She started water boiling for coffee. By candlelight, she went out to pick up the pears that had fallen overnight. She didn't want to get fussed at again. 'Perhaps,' she thought, 'I should just cut those branches back, but I hate to make the tree lopsided.'

It was just beginning to sprinkle when she came back inside. Masoud was up and getting dressed for work. Asah got out a large bowl and the canister of flour.

"I'll get some bread into the oven in just a minute," Asah said as Masoud came into the kitchen to make the coffee.

"Where have you been?" Masoud asked. "Are you wet? Your clothes look damp."

"I just went out to get pears, and it's starting to rain."

"Really?" Masoud looked out the window, although he knew it was too dark to see. "Maybe it's just a passing cloud," he hoped out loud.

While the bread was baking, Masoud and Asah laid their prayer rugs on the floor and said their morning worship and prayers together.

The children were still asleep. Masoud and Asah enjoyed fresh biscuits and coffee together. Asah enjoyed this quiet time with her husband more than any other time of the day.

"Well, I'd better get going," Masoud said. I need to get a lot of work done before the *adhan is called at midday." He skillfully wrapped a turban around his head, grabbed his cloak, kissed his wife, and left. Within seconds, he opened the door again. He said to Asah, "If it keeps raining, pack some things—just in case." Then he was gone.

Asah enjoyed her coffee and solitude before getting the children up. She let them sleep a little longer before she led them in their morning worship. She was also teaching them *Qur'an and *Sunnah at home.

As the morning wore out, it became obvious that the rain was not going to move on. Dark clouds had moved in, and the raindrops were bigger. Asah was not convinced that it would flood, but she had to consider the possibility. She walked about the small house and considered which things she would like most to save. 'Certainly my grandfather's *Qur'an,' she thought. 'And Mama's plate with *Al Fatiha on it.'

Masoud returned in the middle of the day. "Get ready to leave," he told her. "It looks like it could rain for days. Pack whatever we can get, in addition to ourselves, on three camels. I'm going to warn the neighbors. Some of the other men are warning people who live in town." Masoud left, and Asah suddenly became quite concerned.

Asah had already packed some things leisurely, but now it seemed urgent that she hurry. Sensing her alarm, Azhar began to cry. "Don't worry," her big brother comforted her. "Allah will take care of us."

Masoud returned with three borrowed camels. "What about my goats?" Asah asked.

"They won't be able to keep up with us. Put them on the roof and, *insh'Allah, they will survive," answered Masoud.

As they packed the camels, Asah asked Masoud, "Did you warn Maisa?"

"The old woman wouldn't come to the door," answered Masoud.

"Of course not," Asah realized aloud. "She won't speak with men. I'll go."

Asah knocked on Maisa's door, but it did not open. "What do you want?" came a harsh response from inside.

"Maisa, open the door. I have to tell you something."

Finally Maisa opened the door and stood glaring in the doorway.

"Maisa, you have to get out of here. The rain water is building up in the creeks, and we think there may be a flood."

"You stupid, silly girl," spewed old Maisa. "We don't live in a flood area. Leave me alone with your delusions!" Maisa slammed the door.

Asah knocked again. Through the door she called, "Maisa, listen to me. I know this is not a flood area, but it has been flooding in other valleys. People have drowned."

"Go away!"

"Maisa, please. Maisa?" There was no more response from the hateful, old woman. Asah finally said, "Maisa, we're leaving, and I suggest you leave too."

Asah returned to her own house and got the children ready to leave. She dressed them in jackets of camel skin. She hoped the jackets would protect them from the rain now coming down in heavy torrents.

"We must hurry!" Masoud said.

Soon they were traveling with a caravan of camels carrying villagers to the safety of the high mountains. Masoud and Riyad were on one camel, Asah and Azhar were on another, and the bulk of their belongings were on the third camel. Asah glanced back at her goats and said a prayer for them and for stubborn, old Maisa.

From inside her home, Maisa peered from between the heavy curtains that sheltered her from the world she hated. "Stupid people!" she fumed. "I hope they all fall in the river and drown." With a resonate "BAM!" a lightning bolt struck the pear tree and sent a fury of sparks and fire into the air. The window shattered, and Maisa fell back in stunned realization of how terrible the storm.

"Hmmmph." She tried to shake it off. "I've lived through worse than anything you can do," she screamed at the storm. Another bolt of lightning shot from the sky. Flames formed on the roof of a house in the distance. The wind blew the curtains apart and forced Maisa to see the house becoming engulfed in fire and rain.

"You devils, leave me alone," she angrily screamed at imaginary taunts. She sought safety in her bedroom. All around her, however, she could hear the boom and crackle of thunder and fire amidst the pounding torrents. "Stop it," she screamed. "I'm not afraid of you. I'm not afraid of Hell! Take my soul, and I'll give you hell!" she cursed her imagined enemies.

"Ha ha ha ha," voices inside her mind tormented her with their horrible laughter. "Old woman, old woman," they called. "Your soul is already mine. Ha ha ha ha ha."

Maisa screamed a long, shrill cry—not out of fear, but only to try to drown out the voices. Suddenly a wall of water crashed through the bedroom window. It swept through the house, swallowing everything in its path. Old Maisa clung to the top of a table as she was carried out into the street. Waves piled on top of her and tried to hold her down, but she kept bobbing up and cursing the storm.

Unbelief is like fathoms of darkness in deep, vast waters overwhelmed with biflowing waves underneath dense clouds. Such layers of darkness hide even a person's own hand grasping out. If God does not give light, there is no light.

inspired by

Surah 24:40

Finally, her strength nearly depleted, Maisa cried, "Allah! Allah, save me."

But the only response she received was laughter from the voices inside her mind. "Stupid, old woman," the voices said in symphonic tones. "You never called to Allah when you were able to serve Him; why call on Him now? Ha ha ha ha ha."

"I curse you! I cur—" shrieked the old woman before a layer of water again swept over her. She lost her grip on the table. The raging water swirled around her and sucked her underneath into the blackness of certain death.

The voices laughed, and then made a deal: "I can save you, but you must remain forever exactly where I plant your feet."

"Mmmmhuuh," Maisa murmured with her mouth tightly closed against the choking water. Finally she could hold her breath no longer; she gulped in the waters of doom, and then fell unconscious.

Masoud, Asah, and the two children made it safely to the mountain home of Masoud's childhood. The children's grandparents were happy for the unexpected visit, but concerned about the reason. "We will help you rebuild your home if necessary," Masoud's father promised.

After a week, the rain stopped, and the welcome face of the sun smiled on the world. Masoud ventured toward the valley and reported his findings. The valley was indeed flooded, and most of the homes appeared destroyed or badly damaged. The family had to wait several weeks for the floodwaters to subside and the land to become solid once again.

"*AlhamdulAllah," Asah said, "Allah sent a warning, and He spared our lives."

Finally Masoud reported that the family could return home. Once again they packed the camels. They anxiously began the journey. What would be left of their home, they wondered. Asah thought about her goats.

They were saddened, but not surprised, to find that their house, like most of the other houses, was in ruins. The fruit trees and other plants had been swept away. Maisa's house was completely gone. "Poor old Maisa," Asah said, "She never had a chance."

"Baaaaaaaa," came a sound. "Baaaaaaaa."

Asah spun around. "The goats! They survived! But how?"

"Look over there," said Masoud as he pointed. "There's the roof of our house—all in one piece. They must have clung to it for dear life!"

"Allah *held* them to it," Asah said. "They couldn't have fought against the wind and raging waters all alone."

"They must be starving," said Masoud as he reached for the sack of grain kept for the camels.

"Witzh. Witzh," mumbled Azhar.

"What's she talking about?" Masoud asked.

"I don't know," Asah said. She looked toward a hill in the direction Azhar faced. "But I don't remember ever seeing that tree before."

Masoud looked up from feeding the goats. "Hmmph. I don't remember it either, but it was probably there all along and hidden by trees that got swept away in the flood."

"Witzh. Witzh," Azhar continued.

"She's saying *witch*," Riyad said.

Asah stared at the tree as it began to look familiar to her. "Masoud—"

"Hmmm?" he answered.

"Nothing," she said as she shook her head. But she kept looking at that tree. For some reason, it reminded her of Maisa.

Masoud and Asah set up a tent borrowed from Masoud's parents. They began making plans for restoring their home. Their neighbors gradually returned, and the small village turned into a tent city. The people worked together on plans for creating a new village with its own mosque and marketplace. It was a very exciting time.

The people built higher, stronger foundations which, *insh'Allah, could withstand any future floodwaters. They planted fruit trees and grape vineyards, and a community garden was established. An *ummah in a distant city heard of the village's situation.

The distant ummah collected money to be used toward building a mosque for the community. Riyad began memorizing the *Sunnah prayers and the Arabic Qur'an so that he might someday become an *imam.

No one remembered ever having seen the mysterious tree on the hill before. Whenever a rain came, an evil, mournful sound tumbled down the hill and echoed throughout the valley. People were convinced that the sound was coming from the tree. "It is an evil tree like an evil word,"[9] someone said, remembering the Qur'an. The tree's limbs looked like skinny arms ready to grab any unsuspecting passerby. People claimed that they could see an angry face in the tree's trunk. Could it really be old Maisa?

---

[9]Referring to Surah 14: 26.

The Whisper Cat

Prophet Muhammed (peace upon him) loved children and animals. His *Sunnah inspires us to show mercy to all God's creatures.

A baby is always a blessing. Sometimes a baby or older child is orphaned (when his or her parents die). Sometimes the parents are in a bad situation and cannot care for a child. God (blessed and exalted is He) expects believing men and women to insure such a child's welfare. Children are not just the responsibility of their parents; they are the responsibility of a just and moral society. When the expense of generosity and compassion seems beyond our ability, we can trust God to provide for us in amazing and sometimes mysterious ways.

Arabic words to learn:
Allahu akbar (al-la-hoo ak-bar) <u>God is great</u>.
asalam alaiekum (a-sa-lam a-la-ee-kum) <u>Peace be upon you</u>, the universal Muslim greeting.
kufi (koo-fee) Muslim man's prayer cap.
masjid (mas-jid) <u>Mosque</u>, the Muslim house of prayer and worship.
ma'salama (ma-sa-la-ma) <u>With peace</u> (used in bidding farewell).

39

muzien (moo-zeen) The person giving the Muslim call to prayer.
Noor (noor) A female name meaning <u>light</u>.
ramatullah (ra-ma-tul-la) <u>Blessings of God</u>.
salam (sa-lam) <u>Peace</u>.
salat (sa-lat) Prayer and worship.
subhana wa ta'ala (soob-ha-na wa ta-a-la) <u>May He be glorified and exalted</u>, a statement of praise offered after the Name of God.

Hebrew words to learn:
alleluyah (al-la-loo-ya) <u>Praise God</u>.
El Shaddai (el shad-di) <u>God Almighty</u>.
mitzvot (mits-vot) plural of *mitzvah*. Often translated to *good deeds*, but to the Jew an act of mitzvah means much more because the act is a testament to the vitality of the covenant into which Jews have entered with God.

A yellow-orange, evening sun painted the sides of the mosque. The gray-bearded *imam prepared to lead the congregation in prayer and worship. The enchanting call of the *muzien rang out over the rooftops. His voice mingled with the dust aroused by scurrying feet. "Come to *salat! Come to success!" beckoned the muzien from the tall *minaret behind the mosque.

Imam *Yusuf opened the doors to bid welcome to the faithful. He was surprised to find a wooden box on the sunlit, front step of the mosque. The box was covered with a torn, woolen blanket. He lifted the blanket and saw a little bed of straw. A baby, no more than three months old if that, was nestled in the straw bed. The baby was wrapped in a plain linen cloth. Beside her was tucked a note: "If you fear Allah, *subhana wa ta'ala, care for this orphan child."

"What have you there, Imam Yusuf?" With a boom, the familiar voice of Brother *Akbar broke the atmosphere of wonder that had surrounded the imam.

"It's a baby!" declared the imam handing Brother Akbar the note.

"You must honor Allah, subhana wa ta'ala, and find someone to adopt this precious child, Imam."

Allah, subhana wa ta'ala, has entrusted me with this little orphan. I will adopt her myself!" decided the imam. "*Asalam alaiekum," he greeted the people entering the mosque.

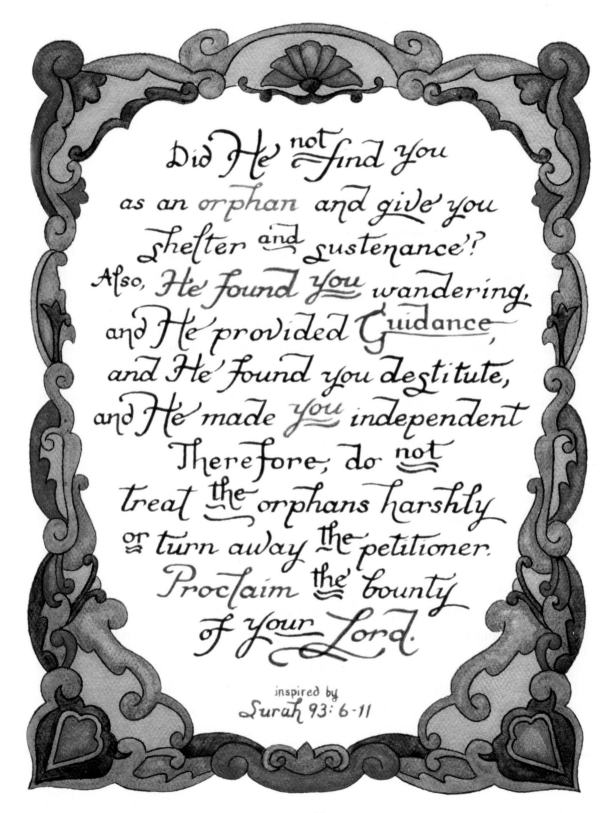

Did He not find you
as an orphan and give you
shelter and sustenance?
Also, He found you wandering,
and He provided Guidance,
and He found you destitute,
and He made you independent
Therefore, do not
treat the orphans harshly
or turn away the petitioner.
Proclaim the bounty
of your Lord.

inspired by
Surah 93: 6-11

"But how will you manage?" asked Brother Akbar. "Your wife has returned to Allah, and the *ummah barely has enough money to support the *masjid and feed the poorest of the community."

"Allah will provide," Imam Yusuf assured him as the people assumed their places for prayer.

As the imam and Brother Akbar walked back into the mosque, Brother Akbar took the baby and asked one of the mothers to care for her during prayer and worship.

"*Allahu akbar; Allaaaahu akbar," Imam Yusuf began the prayers. He led the congregation in the beautiful routine of devotion to God. Afterwards, the imam told the people about the precious bundle. He told them how he had found her at the front door. He told them of his decision to raise the child himself.

Everyone was in awe, and Brother *Tamam stood to speak. "We must help Imam Yusuf with a special gift." He removed his *kufi, dropped in a coin, and passed the hat to the others.

Everyone who could afford it donated a coin or a ring or whatever he or she had. It was far from being enough to clothe and feed a child. The village was a poor one, and families had barely enough for themselves. Still Imam Yusuf was optimistic. "I will name her *Noor*," the imam said, "for she was left in a ray of Allah's golden evening light."

After the final *alhamdulAllah of worship had been said, the girls and women kissed *Noor and asked special blessings on her. The boys and men also wished her *ramatullah. The people bid one another *ma'salama, and soon the imam and Noor were alone.

One of the nursing mothers had given Noor milk. The baby was now content and ready to sleep. Having nothing better for the baby's bed, the imam kept the box of straw and put it beside his cot. It was a cool night, so he covered Noor with his prayer rug.

At dawn, Imam Yusuf was awakened by the sound of the muzein. The imam jumped from his cot. As soon as his feet hit the floor, he realized that the night had gotten much colder than he had expected. 'The baby! Is the baby okay?' he wondered.

Imam Yusuf was more than just a bit surprised to see that Noor was being kept warm by a slinky, little cat sleeping on top of the prayer rug. "From where did you come?" the amazed imam said.

Of course, the imam did not expect an answer. The cat stretched and yawned. She opened her huge eyes, and they looked like polished *jade. Then, in a fuzzy, whispery voice, the cat said, "I came from your wishes, Imam."

Surprised, the imam stared at the cat. He finally decided that he had only imagined that the cat had whispered words. The baby was safe and warm, and that was what mattered.

During morning worship, another of the nursing mothers fed the baby. Throughout the day, Noor was fed at the worship times. Her being fed five times a day became routine, and she grew strong and healthy.

The slinky, strange cat with jade eyes stayed. She kept the baby warm on cool nights. She chased away the field mice who wanted to nest in the baby's bed. Sometimes the imam thought he heard the cat say, "Shooosh, little mice before I have a taste of you." But the imam always dismissed it as being his own silly imagination.

"My old head is playing tricks on me," Imam Yusuf said to the cat. "Your funny, little, whispery noises sound like words to me." The cat simply purred and rubbed against the imam's legs.

When Noor began to outgrow the box bed, the imam thought to buy a cradle. He knew that he only had to ask, and Brother *Ibrahim and Sister *Maryam would give him a cradle from their store. Imam Yusuf was already indebted to everyone's generosity, however, and he did not want to ask for more.

The imam squatted down to look through an old, wooden chest of his belongings to try to find something he could sell. Suddenly, the cat dashed over the top of the chest and startled the imam. Imam Yusuf fell backwards and knocked over the pail he had just filled with the day's supply of water. "What's the matter with you, you crazy, whisper cat!" the imam spouted. Then the imam saw that the cat had in its mouth a green, *brocade pouch.

The cat pounced on the imam's chest and dropped the pouch. In its whispery voice, the cat said, "Here is Noor's treasure; count Allah's blessings!"

The imam opened the pouch. "There's nothing here but rocks!" he said. He was surprised that the pouch contained only round stones. "Why would someone fill such a handsome pouch with plain rocks?" he wondered aloud.

Imam Yusuf went door-to-door. He tried to find the owner of the fine brocade pouch, but no one claimed it. Finally the cat snatched the pouch from the imam's hand and dashed through the streets. "What are you doing now, crazy cat?" the imam called as he ran after the cat. Then the imam stopped and asked himself, "What am I doing, running after a crazy cat?" He turned to go back toward the mosque, but his curiosity urged him. Fussing at himself, he finally headed back after the cat. The cat sat at the edge of town, waiting for the imam to catch up. Then the cat zipped through the orchards and gardens surrounding the town. Imam Yusuf was about to give up the chase. The cat kept luring him by stopping to wait for the imam, so the imam kept after the cat. Finally the cat and the imam were out in the desert. Imam Yusuf was chastising himself out loud. "I must be just as crazy as that cat!" he exclaimed.

The cat gradually slowed down to a determined little prance. Finally she stopped. She looked behind to make sure the imam was paying attention. Then she dropped the brocade pouch into a steep, dark hole. The imam couldn't believe it! Imam Yusuf ran over and looked down into the deep pit. He exclaimed, "You really are a crazy cat! And I must be absolutely insane for following you all the way out here!"

"Hellooooo," a hollow sounding voice rose up out of the pit. "Is someone there?"

Imam Yusuf was stunned with surprise. Finally, he realized the desperate situation and called back. "Yes, I'm here. Are you okay?"

"We're fine, but we can't get out."

"I'll get help," Imam Yusuf promised.

Turning to the cat, Imam Yusuf said, "You wait here and— Aw! Why am I talking to you?" The imam went running, trotting, walking briskly, and finally dragging back to town. By the time he reached the first house, Imam Yusuf was breathless. The sweat of his brow was stinging his eyes, pooling in the corners of his mouth, and dripping from his soft beard.

The family of the house quickly drew cool water from the local well. They presented Imam Yusuf a jar of water and a bowl of dates and allowed him to refresh himself and rest.

After Imam Yusuf had explained the situation, the father of the house addressed his son. "Saddle a camel for Imam Yusuf, and I will find some strong rope."

"*Ilham," Imam Yusuf addressed the little girl quietly occupying a corner. She had etched pictures onto a dry, palm leaf and was using berries to color them. Imam Yusuf said to her, "Will you please go ask Brother Akbar to lead *salat this afternoon? Tell him my salat has feet today." Little Ilham grinned, put aside her craft, and immediately set out to oblige Imam Yusuf's request.

Soon the parents and their son were accompanying Imam Yusuf back out into the desert. The whisper cat still sat marking the spot in the vast sands. A loop was made on one end of the rope and thrown down into the hole. The other end of the rope was tied to the camel's saddle. Soon two dirty and bruised but very grateful boys were pulled from the hole.

"We were searching for *geodes," one boy explained, "when the ground suddenly fell out from under us."

"It's some sort of shaft or old, dry well," the other boy joined in. In his hand, he clutched the green brocade pouch.

"Is that your pouch?" asked Imam Yusuf.

"Yes. It flew from my hand as I began to fall."

The first boy picked up. "Three nights passed, and then the pouch fell in."

"It is filled with geodes?" the imam asked.

"Yes," the boy clutching the pouch verified. "My father is a jewelry craftsman, and he slices, polishes, and mounts small geodes for the wonderful crystals inside."

"I should have recognized them myself," the imam confessed. "Geodes look ordinary on the outside. I had forgotten the beauty inside them. *Allah has prepared this treasure for those who seek it. That is much the way of the *Qur'an. It may look like an ordinary book for those who do not know of the beauty inside, but those who seek will discover the miracle. Allah, *subhana wa ta'ala, provides signs in nature. The geode is one of His many signs."

The assisting family offered their home to the two boys until morning. Imam Yusuf then escorted them back to their parents.

With the loan of camels, the boys and Imam Yusuf set out shortly after morning worship. As they neared the Jewish village where the boys lived, one of the boys spotted a poster. "Look, that's us!" he said.

The other boy read the poster aloud. "Missing. Yechiel Borfman and Isaac Eckstein. Reward."

"I wonder how much we're worth," Isaac said with a chuckle.

From the window of the house, Yechiel's mother saw the camels approaching. She immediately recognized her son. The mother dropped the plate she held in her hand. She dashed out of the house and ran, arms wide open. She scooped her son into her arms as he slid from the camel he shared with Isaac. "*Alleluyah! Alleluyah!" she cried, and she clutched him tightly against her.

"You're smothering me, Mother," Yechiel protested.

Isaac directed the imam toward the Eckstein household. Isaac was also happily greeted. The Ecksteins invited Imam Yusuf into their home and offered refreshments. They eagerly listened to the entire story of the boys' and the imam's adventures.

After the long story was finished, Isaac's father told the imam, "I am sure you will be able to use the reward to provide for your precious Noor."

"Oh, no!" Imam Yusuf protested. "Other than the eternal reward Allah promises, I could never accept a reward for a good deed. Good deeds should always be done in the name of Allah, subhana wa ta'ala."

"Then consider this among *my* *mitzvot, Imam," Brother Eckstein insisted. He dumped the geodes from the brocade pouch. Then he refilled the pouch with a generous amount of coins. "This is my way of glorifying *El Shaddai for blessing us with the safe return of Isaac and his friend."

Imam Yusuf humbly accepted the pouch of coins. He bade farewell, and then mounted one camel. Leading the other camel, the imam began the trek back to his own village.

That night, Imam Yusuf tucked Noor into her small, box bed. The cat snuggled over Noor's feet and whispered, "Count Allah's blessings; buy Noor a cradle."

"I don't believe cats can whisper," said Imam Yusuf, "but I believe in Allah's blessings. Tomorrow I will shop for a cradle."

47

The Ali Mystery

The Qur'an offers guidance for every detail of a believer's life and for the community as a whole. For example, it advises on leaving a will and even what to do if someone thinks the will is wrong. "The Ali Mystery" is about a will that wasn't clear. Sometimes God's guidance also seems unclear, but, as the story shows, even the obscure is explained in obvious ways when we look for the right signs.

Hebrew words to learn:
shalom (sha-lom) <u>Peace.</u>
shalom alekhem (sha-lom a-le-kh'em) <u>Peace be upon you.</u>

Ali ibn Ali had three sons named after him: Ali, his brother Ali, and his other brother *Ali. When Ali *ibn Ali died, he left a will as prescribed by the *Qur'an. "I leave all my earthly possessions," stated the will, "to be shared equally by my sons Ali and Ali, but not Ali." But which two Ali's did he intend to receive the inheritance? No one was sure. The Qur'an warns against bickering and injustice, so the Ali brothers asked their *imam how to go about solving the mystery.

"There is a very wise, old *sage who lives in the hills near the village where Ali ibn Ali was born. Go ask his advice," said the imam.

Ali, his brother Ali, and his other brother Ali packed food and water onto their donkeys and began their journey. After they had traveled some distance, they stopped to rest and to refresh themselves with water and dates. Ali noticed tracks in the sand and said, "Look; a donkey has traveled here just a short time ago. Its tracks are still fresh, and they lead in that direction." He motioned with a nod of the head.

His brother Ali said, "It must have been carrying sugar."

"And salt," his other brother Ali added.

Ali said, "It appears that the donkey is blind in one eye."

After they had continued their journey, a man on foot approached them. "Have you seen a donkey on the loose?" he asked.

"Does it have only one good eye?" asked Ali.

"Yes!" happily replied the man.

"Is it carrying sugar and salt?" asked the brother Ali.

"Yes, that's her!" The man was quite glad.

"Do you know the bags have holes in them?" asked the other brother Ali.

"Where is she?" asked the man.

"We haven't seen her," informed Ali, and he nudged his donkey to go on.

"What do you mean you haven't seen her?" the man asked with a tone of confusion and aggravation.

"I think she went that way," said the brother Ali as he pointed.

"You should hurry to catch up with her before her tracks are blown away," said the other brother Ali.

The man did not believe that the brothers had not seen his donkey, so he ran after them and shouted insults at them.

A *rabbi was coming toward them on his way to teach at a *synagogue.

"*Asalam alaiekum," said Ali and his brother Ali and his other brother Ali.

"*Shalom alekhem," returned the rabbi.

Everyone introduced himself, and then the man looking for his donkey told the rabbi, "These men have taken my donkey, and they won't tell me where she is."

"We haven't seen his donkey," calmly stated Ali.

"They described her to me," the man insisted. "They told me that she has only one eye and that she was carrying sugar and salt. They must have seen her!"

"But that's all we know about the donkey," said the brother Ali.

"We know which direction she took, but we haven't seen her," said the other brother Ali.

"Then please explain how you know that the donkey has only one eye and is carrying sugar and salt," begged the rabbi.

"We saw the donkey's tracks in the sand," explained Ali. "We noticed that only the grass to one side had been eaten. We thought that the donkey must be blind in one eye."

"We saw a stream of white crystals covered with ants," explained the brother Ali. "We thought that the donkey must be carrying sugar."

"But there was also a stream of white crystals without ants," explained the other brother Ali. "We figured that must be salt."

50

"That settles it!" decided the rabbi. "These men have not seen your donkey—not Ali, not Ali, and not Ali."

After a mumbled apology, the man went in the direction that Ali had said the donkey went.

Later in the day, the brothers came upon a *Bedouin tribe camped beside a small pool. As was customary, the Bedouin Arabs invited the strangers for coffee. The brothers Ali relaxed. They explained to the Bedouin *sheik about the confusion of their father's will.

"I have a suggestion," said the sheik. "My grandmother is very ill. If one of you can make her feel better, that one should be one Ali to whom inheritance is granted. If one of you can cure her, that one should be the other Ali."

The brothers agreed that this would be a fair way to settle the misunderstanding.

Ali went out and gathered various herbs to make a medicinal tea. The grandmother drank the tea, but it only made her sick at her stomach.

His brother Ali collected leaves and made a poultice for her head. It made her skin hot, and she broke out in a rash.

His other brother Ali made a medicine stick from old bones and feathers. He shook the stick over her and chanted some senseless words. It scared the old woman so much that she died.

Furious, the Bedouin sheik shouted, "That settles it! None of you deserves the inheritance—not Ali, not Ali, and not Ali!"

Gulping their pride, the Ali brothers promptly left.

Finally they arrived at their father's hometown. They asked directions for finding the famous sage.

The brothers went to the cave wherein the sage lived. They greeted the sage and explained their problem. The sage pondered for a few minutes. Finally he asked, "If you could have for yourself anything from your father, for what would you wish, and why?"

"I would wish for his heart," Ali stated, "because he was kind and generous. He helped anyone in need."

His brother Ali decided, "I would wish for his mind, because he was wise and able to provide guidance to anyone who came to him."

Without hesitation, his other brother Ali blurted, "I'd like to have his liver, because mine is diseased from too much whiskey."[10]

A bit shocked, the sage declared, "That settles it! The inheritance belongs to Ali and Ali, but not Ali!"

---

[10]Muslims believe it is wrong to indulge in the consumption of alcoholic beverages. The Qur'an says, "(Your followers) question you [Muhammed] concerning intoxicants [alcohol and drugs] and gambling. Say, 'In them are harm and some benefit to Humanity, but the harm is greater that the benefit'" (inspired by Surah 2: 219). A little wine or brandy is believed to aid in digestion, help blood circulation, and help induce a restful night's sleep, but use of alcohol generally leads to dependency (alcoholism) and drunkenness which leads to violence, poor judgment, social misconduct, family problems, poverty, and moral ruin. Alcoholism also causes health problems like liver cirrhosis and brain cell degeneration. Similarly, drugs are of great value for medical purposes, but the effects of harmful substances are disastrous. When a pregnant woman uses drugs, alcohol, or tobacco, especially during the first five weeks of pregnancy (usually before she even knows she is pregnant), the child can suffer devastating, life-long physical and mental defects. Use of harmful substances by a woman who is or who may become pregnant can doom a child to facing a life of unfair, constant struggle. Muslims also consider gambling to be wrong although there can be some benefit. In today's society, the public lottery is a great source of income for the state, but it ruins individuals who become addicted and foolishly deplete the cash reserves intended for the families' welfare.

The Ghost Camels of Amal

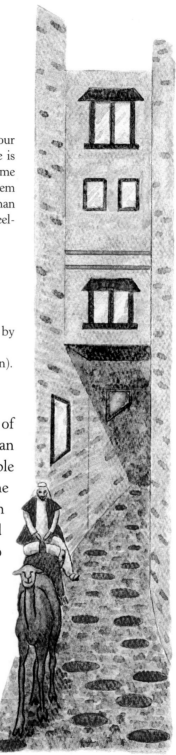

It is written in the Qur'an, "O Humanity, there has come from your Sovereign Lord direction and a cure for your spiritual diseases. There is guidance and mercy for those who believe" (inspired by Surah 10: 57). Some people, however, have too much pride, arrogance, and anger. They seem unable to make room for God's grace and mercy. This is the story of a man who went on a journey. His experience caused him to get rid of the bad feelings in his life. He finally presented his soul as an empty vessel to God.

Arabic words to learn:
abooya (ab-oo-ya) <u>My father</u>.
amal (a-mal) <u>Hope</u>.
ibnee (ib-nee) <u>My son</u>.
Ka'bah (ka-ba) The House of God believed to have been built by Abraham and Ishmael in Meccah, Saudi Arabia. (See footnote #3.)
keef halak? (keef hal-ak) <u>How are you?</u> to a man (*keef halik* to a woman).

Very far away in time and space was the Land of *Amal. Five times a day the *adhan was called by an ancient, blind *muzein. The old muzein was so feeble that he could barely climb the steps to the top of the *minaret. He was always cheerful and greeted everyone with God's blessings. He was well known for bubbling with good advice and wise sayings. He always had time to listen to anyone's problems.

He was on his way to the street market to buy bread. He heard the soft 'cluff cluff' of an approaching camel. He stopped at the edge of the street to greet the traveler. "*Asalam alaiekum," he shouted merrily. "*Keef halak?"

"*Salam," mumbled a stranger's voice.

"I hope that you are happy on this glorious day that *Allah has made!" declared the muzein.

"What's so glorious about it?" challenged a grumpy voice. The 'cluff cluff' came to a halt. "The sun is just as hot, the dust is just as dirty, and the wind is just as harsh as every other day. What is there to be happy about?"

"Allah is good and merciful," answered the old muzein. "Does that not make you joyful?"

The muzein heard the gentle whack of a stick against the camel's skin. He knew that meant that the stranger had signaled the camel to kneel. The sound of sandals scuffled on the hard-packed sand. The muzein could tell that the stranger had dismounted.

The stranger's voice was nearer now. "How should I know anything of Allah's goodness and mercy? My employees keep asking for more money for less work. The cost of materials keeps going up and cutting into my profits. My wife wants a bigger house, and I'm still paying for the house we have now!"

"These material things are not what's important," said the muzein. "Give your finest possessions to the poor and be happy living modestly. Glorify Allah by deeds of charity and kindness, and He will reward you with the peace that is missing from your life."

"I'd like to have that peace, but not by giving away my hard-earned money. I want to keep my money and still be happy! I have searched all my life for paradise, but I can never find it. Every day is just another struggle for a dollar and just another struggle for a morsel of food. Every day I must struggle to keep my business partners from cheating me."

The muzein sighed. He felt tired. He plopped his bony bottom right there by the road. The stranger lowered his own body and rested on his knees.

"If I could find paradise, perhaps I could at least be as happy as that camel," said the stranger, with a nod toward his camel. "He does not concern himself with charity and good deeds, but he is always smiling as if he knows some secret to happiness."

"I cannot see him," replied the blind muzein, "but I know that he is smiling. It is said that the camel smiles because he alone knows the one hundredth name."

"About what are you talking, old man?"

"Do you know the ninety-nine names of Allah?"[11] asked the muzein.

---

[11]The Qur'an gives 99 names or titles for God.

"Yes, I learned them as a child when I spent summers with my grandmother. Are you saying that the camel knows the one hundredth name of Allah?"

"So it is said," answered the muzein.

"Do you think that I could find my paradise if I discovered what the camel knows?" eagerly asked the stranger.

"I think," advised the muzein, "that the more you learn of Allah, the happier you will be."

"How can I learn such things?" asked the stranger impatiently.

"Be faithful in *salat and study the Qur'an."

"I have no time for religious routines. Give me a simple solution," insisted the stranger. "What about that one hundredth name?"

"I have heard of a way to learn the hundredth name," said the muzein, "but it is very dangerous."

"I fear nothing!" boasted the stranger. "Tell me what to do."

"When I was a boy," began the muzein, "long before I became blind, my father took me to the top of Mount Amal. It was just after a spring rain. The climb was steep and strenuous. It was late afternoon when we reached the peak. Puffs of steam were rolling up from the hot, damp sands far below us. My father had packed a skin of water, some dried fish and bread, and a blanket roll. We snuggled under the blanket and shared the fish and bread. As we ate, the steam formed into clouds, and the clouds formed shapes.

"'Look, *Abooya,' I said, 'the clouds look like camels.'

"'Yes,' my father said. 'There is a legend that after the first spring rain, one hundred ghost camels encircle Mount Amal. Each one bears one of the ninety-nine names of Allah, except one. There is one ghost camel that is grinning so widely that his teeth gleam in the sun. That camel will give you a hint about the one hundredth name of Allah.'

"'But, Abooya,' I implored, 'What if I want more than a hint? What if I want the full knowledge of the one hundredth name?'

"'I don't suggest that you try it, *Ibnee, but I have heard of a way. A person must leap from the Flat Rock of Amal and jump onto the back of the grinning camel. That camel will tell the person the hundredth name.' My father pointed to a huge slab of flat rock hovering over a straight drop."

The stranger simply asked, "Didn't it rain here this morning?"

"Yes, it did," replied the old muzein.

Nothing else was said between the two men. The stranger got up, mounted his camel, and rode away.

"It's silly superstition," the stranger told himself as his camel plodded along. "He's just a crazy, old man. I don't have time to climb a mountain. It's a ridiculous idea."

The stranger was still arguing with himself when he arrived at the base of Mount Amal. "I'm not really going to do this, am I?" But something kept edging him on. Finally, he took his blanket roll, a flask of water, a crust of bread, and a piece of camel jerky from his pack. He then began toiling up the steep cliff.

The mountain peak was just as the old muzein had described. The stranger curled up in his blanket, directly on the flat rock. The hard punch of wind gusts made the man feel like an unwelcome guest. The mists from the rain were already traveling up the mountain from the sun-heated sands below. As the man chewed morsels of bread and jerky, the ghost camels began to form. Soon the camels were smiling and making a mysterious *circumnavigation around the mountain—like the journey made around the *Ka'bah. The man watched the camels closely as the wind whispered: "...the Manifest, the Aware, the Great, the Responsive, the All-Seeing, the All-Hearing,...." As the camels traveled faster, the whispers blended into one sound, one sonnet, one prayer of nature.

At last the unhappy man saw a sparkle from a distant camel. As the camel came nearer, the man could clearly see that it was grinning. The man stood on the edge of the flat rock. He was trembling with fear. When the grinning, ghost camel was directly beneath him, the man hurled himself over the edge of the rock.

The man was moving in mid-air. The clouds were so thick that he couldn't see beyond them. He didn't even realize that his cloak had gotten hung on a thorny limb jutting from the cliff. The gusty wind bouncing his body made him feel as if he were moving. His cloak billowed like a balloon as it hugged the upward-moving wind. The man thought that he was encircling the mountain on the back of the grinning ghost camel.

"Tell me the hundredth name," demanded the man. But there was no sound but the haunting, mysterious orchestra of whispering winds. "I demand to know the hundredth name!"

Within the sound of the orchestra, names were echoed: "...the Creator, the Giver of Life, the Giver of Death, the Resurrector...." But the hundredth name could not be heard.

As the man became exhausted and desperate, his demands turned into pleading. "Please tell me the hundredth name. I beg you to tell me." For hours he begged, and moaned, and cried.

Darkness began to creep into the clouds. The man's fingers and toes were becoming numb from the damp, cold air gripping the mountain. Finally, he wanted nothing more than to just be gone from there. He realized, however, that the muzein had never mentioned how to dismount from a ghost camel.

"I want off," he whined. "Carry me to the flat rock, and let me down." But the camel did not respond.

The man stretched his hands through the thick, white mist. He hoped to find something onto which to grab, but there was nothing but air. "Take me back to the mountain. Please!" he continued to beg as he bounced within the clouds while the wind whipped him.

Finally black darkness and intense cold joined the cloud camels as they taunted the man. In his mind, he was still circling the mountain. In reality, he was only dangling from the thorny branch.

"This must be a bit like Hell," he thought aloud. "Allah is all around me, yet I feel so far from Him. I cannot feel His grace, His mercy, His compassion."

Echoes continued around him: "...the Powerful, the Protector, the Provider...."

The man was filled with dread as he wondered if this nightmarish adventure would ever end. When he was drained of all his own strength and resources, he had nothing left but the power of prayer.

"Allah," he said aloud, "the Most Gracious, the Most Merciful, the One Worthy of All Praise. You are the Kind and Righteous One. You are the Forgiver, and I am the sinner. You are the Guide, and I am the lost. You are the Restorer, and I am the one in despair."

All night the man prayed, prostrated upon the wind. As he prayed, his anger, his greed, his impatience, his vain pride—they all melted and fell from him like raindrops from heavy clouds.

He began to remember prayers his grandmother had taught him. "O Sovereign Lord, let your forgiveness shelter us—me, my family, and all believers—on the day that justice will be established. Our Sovereign Lord, do not condemn us for our transgressions, and do not give us such difficult assignments as those martyrs who went before us. Our Sovereign Lord, do not call us to perform more spiritual duties than we are capable of. Blot out our sins, grant us forgiveness, and be merciful to us. You are our Protector. Help us against those who challenge our faith."[12]

After many hours of prayers, the man began to feel peace settle into the empty vessel of his soul. His spiritual darkness was replaced with "the Light." His distress was replaced with "the Source of Peace." His weakness was replaced with "the Strong One." His hatred was replaced with "the Loving One." His sinful nature was replaced with "the Righteous One."

Morning finally came. As the day became warmer, the heavy mists grew thinner and began to dissipate. The man could see glimpses of the village below. The camel he was riding began fading away. The winds howled as they roared even more strongly up the steep mountainside. The gusts hit the man's body hard. He felt as if he were being beaten with blows from a raging beast. He tightly closed his eyes and cried to God for help. "Allah. Allah. You are the Avenger and the Watchful. You are the One who Humiliates and the One who Sustains. In You I trust. Allah. Allah. Allah."

Suddenly the force of the wind snapped the branch clutching the man's cloak. Air filled the cloak and made it billow like a balloon. The wind blew so hard that it thrust the man upward. The wind hurled the man to the safety of the flat rock. The man was so thankful that he prostrated there and quickly praised God. He then bounded down the steep, rocky descent. The man made his way as fast as possible down the rough terrain. He finally had to sit down and catch his breath.

"Did you find that for which you were looking?" a familiar voice asked.

---

[12]Inspired by Surah 3: 147 and Surah 2: 286.

The man was surprised to see the old muzein. But he looked different somehow. Perhaps it was only because of the sun shining directly behind him. The man was partially blinded by looking toward the now-blazing sun. The muzein's image seemed painted into its brightness.

"Yes, I did," answered the man solemnly. "I found my paradise, and it was with me all along."

"Perhaps in your paradise the hundredth name of Allah is 'the One who Loves Souhail ibn Sariyah,'" the muzein responded, saying the man's name.

The muzein continued up the mountain as the man pondered the thought. Suddenly he jumped up and shouted after the old man. "Wait! How did you know my name?" But the muzein was already gone.

Souhail thought that was very strange. He wondered why the old man had ventured up the steep mountain all alone when he was in such frail condition.

Souhail finally arrived back at the village. He went to the street market to inquire about the old man. "Do you know the old, blind man who lives here?" he asked a vendor.

"Oh, yes," replied the vendor. "Everyone knew and loved the muzein."

"Why are you speaking of him in the past tense?" asked Souhail.

"He died last night," answered the vendor. "His body was found this morning, still prostrated in *salat. It was his habit to often spend an entire night in salat at the *masjid. It was fitting that the angels took his soul at such a time."

Souhail was too bewildered to ask any more questions. He simply went to the mosque and knelt in prayer on behalf of his friend, the old muzein.

As he left the mosque, Souhail emptied his money pouch. He put all he had with him into the collection box for the poor. He refreshed his camel, and then headed back home. He wanted to tell his wife and children the story of his night on the mountain. The legend of the ghost camels of Mount Amal and the traveler's story were told over and over. Everyone was amazed by the story of Souhail ibn Sariyah, which means *a star, the son of clouds at night.*

Noor and the Rude Awakening

It is recorded that Jesus (peace upon him, and may he bring peace) taught a message called "the Sermon on the Mount." The sermon included the Beatitudes: "Blessed are those who realize their spiritual needs; the Kingdom of Heaven belongs to them. Blessed are those who mourn; God will comfort them. Blessed are those who are humble; they will receive God's promises. Blessed are those whose greatest desire is to do what God requires of them; God will satisfy them completely. Blessed are those who are merciful to others; God will be merciful to them. Blessed are the pure in heart; they will see God. Blessed are those who strive for peace; they will be called God's spiritual children. Blessed are those who are persecuted for the sake of God; the Kingdom of Heaven belongs to them" (inspired by Matthew 5: 3-10). Those who follow the opposite path, however, are in for a rude awakening!

Arabic words to learn:

La illaha illa Allah; Muhammedan rasulAllah (la il-la-ha il-la Al-la; mu-ham-med-an ra-sool-al-la) The Muslim confession of faith (called *shahada*): <u>There is no god but God; Muhammed is the messenger of God</u>.
du'a (doo-ah) Personal <u>prayer</u>.
kutba (koot-ba) <u>Sermon</u>.
marhaba (mar-ha-ba) <u>Hello</u>.
tafaddalee (ta-fad-da-lee) <u>Please</u>, when extending an invitation to a female (to a male, *tafaddal*).

The mosque was the only home *Noor had ever known. She had been abandoned there as an infant. She had been raised by Imam Yusuf, a kind widower who had devoted his life to serving God and providing for Noor. When Noor was fourteen years old, Imam Yusuf became very sick. Noor held Imam Yusuf's hand. She told him that she loved him and would miss him. She sang to him, "*La illaha illa Allah; Muhammedan rasul Allah" and the words of "* Al Fatiha." Finally he began his journey to Heaven.

The new *imam and his wife allowed Noor to keep her small room in the back of the mosque. The imam and his family were kind to Noor, but she was lonely. She missed her adoptive father terribly. The *ummah had helped care for Noor, but she did not have very close friends. She was a quiet, pensive girl. She spent most of her time alone, drawing, writing poetry, and making clothes for the poor. Her constant companion was Whisper, a funny, little cat. The cat made whispery sounds that only Noor could understand. Imam Yusuf had understood them too, but he never liked to admit it. When Noor was little, she told people what the cat was saying. People thought she was playing a pretend game. When she got older, however, people began to think she might be crazy. She finally learned to keep secret her conversations with Whisper.

Noor found solice in tending the mosque and saying prayers. She said the *Sunnah prayers five times a day, and her *du'a never ceased. Noor kept the mosque swept and dusted. She even repaired cracks in the marble floor and replaced damaged tiles and peeling wallpaper. Sometimes she felt resentment toward this new family that had moved into her space and taken over Imam Yusuf's duties. Noor had to remind herself that the mosque belonged to God and the ummah, not to her. Now a year had passed since Imam Yusuf's death. Noor began to feel that her place in the mosque was slipping away. She felt like a guest whose visit was over, but she had no place else to go.

Much had changed in Noor's village in the past few years. A large vein of silver had been discovered. It was on public lands, so the *Sultan controlled all assets. The Sultan was a fair man. He used the money to help the community. He worked to provide better opportunities for education and jobs. The standard of living greatly improved for most people. It was a good time. People had plenty to eat. They could afford things that made their lives more enjoyable. It was also a loving community, and Noor was content there.

The tranquility quickly began to change, however. An evil wind blew across the land. Riding the wind were three evil *jinn. Their names were Arrogance, Greed, and Gossip. Arrogance crept into people's homes and whispered, "Allah chose you to receive the riches you have. That proves that you are better than other people. Have nothing to do with those less fortunate than you. It is their own fault that they lack the same success as you."

Greed held tightly to everyone's money and whispered, "You have the right to this money. You are the one who has worked hard for it. You are the one who should benefit

63

from it. Let others take care of themselves. If someone is in need, it's his or her own fault; it's not your problem."

Gossip stayed close to people's ears, pointed at everyone, and said, "Look there. That looks suspicious."

Arrogance, Greed, and Gossip carried out their evil deeds. The community became divided. Some people became snobs. They considered themselves better than anyone different from what they considered proper. Many people became victims of mean and unfair treatment. The greedy people saved their money all for themselves. They used dishonest ways to become richer. They had no concern for the poor. Almost everyone became the victim of gossip. People constantly criticized one another. They invented tales based on rumors and false ideas.

Noor silently observed the community. It became more evil and corrupt. More and more people stopped coming to the mosque for *salat. Finally there was only a small group of faithful believers. Noor was basically a quiet, shy person, but she felt that she

The Three Evil Jinn

must do something. She wanted to save the community from the evil jinn. The new imam was a good man, but he was not as wise as Imam Yusuf had been. Imam Yusuf had constantly helped people. It had taken him many years to gain respect. The new imam was still trying to gain such respect.

"What can I do?" Noor asked Whisper. "I cannot just sit here and watch the community stray farther and farther from Allah. If Imam Yusuf were here, he would do something, so, *insh'Allah, I must do something on his behalf."

"Go to the Sultan," Whisper said in scratchy, whispery sounds. "Tell him your ideas."

"I don't have any ideas," Noor said.

"You will at the right time," whispered the cat.

Noor had always trusted the cat. Imam Yusuf had called Whisper "a *jinni cat." Whisper's talking had led Noor and Imam Yusuf to make many good decisions. But this time Noor was not so sure. Why would the Sultan even speak to her, a simple orphan girl? "Well, it won't hurt to try," Noor decided.

Noor packed a travel bag with a shoulder strap. She and Whisper set out on their own to see the Great Sultan.

The Kingdom of Sultan *Nabeeh was quite a distance across the country. Noor and Whisper walked all day. When they came to a nice grove of trees, they decided to camp there and refresh themselves. Noor had packed some bread and a flask of water. She and Whisper were eating when three Christian *nuns riding on donkeys came by. They were on their way to care for a sick family. Even though Noor had brought only enough food for herself and Whisper, she invited the nuns to stop and share her food. The nuns agreed and accepted a little bread. They brought out a linen cloth and unfolded it. The nuns unpacked dates, raisins, and dried pears to share. Noor had plenty, and Whisper caught some grasshoppers to eat.

"What is a young girl like you doing out here all alone?" asked a nun with a serious look.

Noor explained the troubles in her community and how she and Whisper had decided to seek the help of the Sultan.

"Ahhhh, so you are not alone," said a nun with an aura of wisdom about her. "The spirit of Jesus walks with one who seeks peace and goodness."

One who leaves home
for the service of God
will find many places
on the earth
for refuge and assistance.

inspired by
Surah 4:100

"May we give you some advice?" asked a soft-spoken nun.

Noor was happy to have any help at all.

"Think of Jesus as your big brother looking out for you," advised the nun. "Jesus said, 'Whoever serves the Heavenly Guardian is my sister.'"[13]

The wise-looking nun said, "Have great faith. Jesus promised, 'I assure you that if you have faith even as big as a tiny mustard seed, you can do anything.'"[14]

"Add perseverance to your faith," said the nun with the serious look. "Jesus said, 'Whoever perseveres until the end will be saved.'"[15]

"And Jesus was sent by Allah to guide us to salvation," the soft-spoken nun added.

Noor told them of Prophet Muhammed (peace upon him). "The messenger to our people said, 'Whoever believes in the One True God—and that Muhammed is His messenger; and that Jesus is Allah's servant, His messenger, His Word breathed into Mary, and a spirit emanating from Allah; and that Paradise and Hell are real—shall be received by Allah into Heaven.'"[16]

"Ahhhhh," the nuns said in unison.

"Then your messenger was very wise indeed," said the wise-looking one.

Noor smiled, and her face glowed.

The nuns prayed for Noor, blessed her, and then said farewell. They left to continue their journey. Noor and Whisper prepared for the evening worship.

Noor finally lay down to sleep on the blanket she had brought. She thought of the nuns and pondered their advice.

Noor was too far from any mosque to be able to hear the *adhan, so she guessed at the time. She said the morning prayer, and then went back to sleep. She was still tired from the long walk the day before, and the daylight was still too dim for traveling. She

---

[13]Inspired by Matthew 12: 50.
[14]Inspired by Matthew 17: 20.
[15]Inspired by Matthew 24: 13.
[16]A hadith reported by Bukhari.

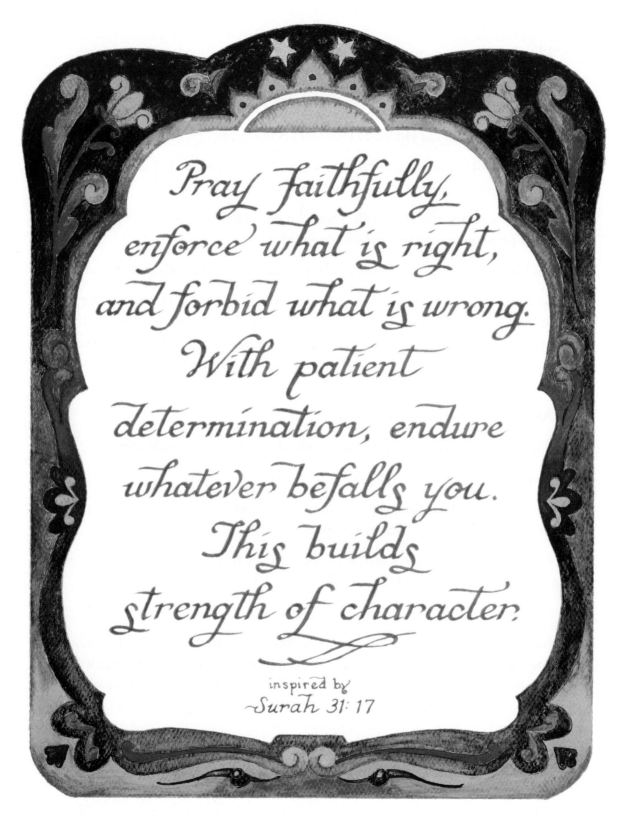

Pray faithfully,
enforce what is right,
and forbid what is wrong.
With patient
determination, endure
whatever befalls you.
This builds
strength of character.

inspired by
Surah 31: 17

waited until the long shadows of morning had risen from their prayers, and then Noor and Whisper stretched and got up. They ate some bread, and then packed up and continued their journey.

About midday, they came upon a tent. "*Shalom," called a friendly voice. "Come, little one, have some fish and wine."

Noor approached the camper. "*Salam," she returned his greeting.

"*Tafadalee, tafadalee," he invited. "Sit here and rest awhile."

Noor noticed wares in a cart, and she saw that a donkey had been unhitched and allowed to graze. She realized that the man must be a traveling peddler. Noor sat down in front of the tent. She shared her bread with him and accepted his offer of dried fish. She politely refused the wine. Of course, he wanted to know where she was headed and why, and she shared her story.

"*Alleluyah," the Jew said after hearing of her intent.

"*AlhamdulAllah," Noor responded.

"Let me give you some advice," the Jew volunteered. Noor nodded. She was surprised that Whisper had curled up in the Jew's lap. Whisper seemed to be familiar with the Jewish man.

"Concerning arrogance," the Jew began, "a proverb of King Solomon says, 'People who are proud will soon be disgraced. It is wise to be modest.'[17] Concerning greed, a proverb says, 'Be generous, and you will prosper. Help others, and you will receive help.'[18] And another says, 'Riches will do you no good on the day you face death, but honesty can save your life.'[19] And of gossip, Solomon said, 'The gossip of evil people does as much harm as murder, but the words of the righteous rescue those who are threatened.'"[20]

The Jew gently put his hand to Noor's face. "You, little one," he said, "will be blessed for your *mitzvot." Noor thought that light seemed to emanate from the Jew's

---

[17]Inspired by Proverbs 11: 2.
[18]Inspired by Proverbs 11: 25.
[19]Inspired by Proverbs 11: 4.
[20]Inspired by Proverbs 12: 6.

face as he quoted another proverb. "Remember this," he said, "'A lie has a short life, but truth lives on forever. Those who plan evil are in for a rude awakening, but the one who works for good will find happiness.'"[21]

Noor said, "My Holy Book also speaks of the wisdom of King Solomon." The Jew was pleased to know that.

Noor thought that the Jew could have quoted proverbs all day, but she had to keep walking. She fondly bade him farewell.

She walked all afternoon, stopping only for prayers and short rest periods. She was almost to the Kingdom of Sultan Nabeeh when she saw a bald man in a burgundy-red robe coming toward her. As he walked, he swept the road in front of him. Noor thought this was very strange. "*Marhaba," she said shyly.

The man smiled and nodded, but continued his sweeping.

Noor had come to the conclusion that everyone she met on her journey must have some advice for her, so she explained to the strange, little man, "I am going to the Sultan to ask for help to end the arrogance, greed, and gossip in my community. Do you have some advice for me?"

The man reached down and petted Whisper's head. "Why do you ask my advice?" he asked Noor. "You have the answers within yourself."

Noor silently pondered his remark as he walked past her, gently sweeping in front of himself. Noor thought how odd this man seemed. She wanted to have some understanding of his strange behavior. She walked behind him and said, "I am not a rude child, but if you don't mind, I would really like to know why you are sweeping the road."

"I am on my way to consult a very wise Buddhist *sage who contemplates on the high mountain," he explained. "I want my spirit to be pure when I reach him, so I do not want to be guilty of destroying life on my journey."

Noor wrinkled her forehead with confusion. For one thing, she had never heard of a *Buddhist. "But what does that have to do with your sweeping?" she asked.

The monk stopped and looked at her as if she had no understanding at all. "Are there not tiny insects traveling along the same road? We are all parts of one life. To

---

[21]Inspired by Proverbs 12: 19-20.

destroy even the smallest, living creature is to destroy a part of ourselves." The man continued on his way. He gently swept the path in front of him in order to move aside any tiny ant or beetle on which he might otherwise step.

Noor watched him slowly proceed on his tedious journey. She thought how strangely wonderful it was for someone to consider even God's tiniest creatures. She turned and continued on her way in the opposite direction. Now she carefully looked at the road before placing each step.

It was nearly dusk when Noor reached the city. It seemed so big and busy. She walked along the street market as she waited for the *adhan. Soon the voice of the *muzein was hurled across the buildings and through the streets and alleys. Noor and Whisper quickly walked in the direction of the *minaret from which the sound came.

Noor walked into the spacious, open court of the mosque. She located the women's area and unfurled her prayer rug. Women and girls quickly surrounded her. They greeted her with kisses on her cheeks. She felt right at home. The girls had plenty of affection for Whisper also.

Between prayers and Qur'anic recitations, Noor explained to the women why she had come. She also told them about the adventures of her journey.

"You must speak to the imam," one of the women told her. "After the first session of salat, Imam *Nawfal will be available for advice. He will speak with anyone who seeks his counsel."

Noor did as the women suggested, and the imam was happy to see her. He was impressed that she had made the long journey alone in order to seek a cure for her community's spiritual illnesses.

"I will see that you are admitted into the presence of the Sultan," promised the imam. "Come tomorrow—wait—where are you staying?"

Noor explained that she had no arrangements, so the imam asked one of the men nearby to get Brother *Raatib.

"Brother Raatib," the imam asked, "would your wife be willing to take in this child for a few days? She has come to see the Sultan."

"Certainly, Imam Nawfal," Raatib assured.

"AlhamdulAllah," Noor softly whispered, and the whisper cat echoed her praises. Noor was amazed at how God had insured her safety throughout the journey. He had provided food and good counsel. Now He had insured for her a place to stay and even an appearance before the Sultan.

"I will send someone for you when the Sultan is ready to see you," Imam Nawfal told Noor.

Noor said her morning prayer in the tiny room she was given at the home of Brother Raatib. His lovely wife *Afrah wafted in with dates, baklava, and tea. Noor got dressed, but she sat in a chair and drifted off to sleep again. She felt as if she could sleep for a week.

"Wake up, Noor," a sweet voice whispered, and Noor was gently shaken awake.

"Where am I? Oh, I remember." Noor had been sleeping so soundly that Afrah's voice seemed to have brought Noor back from some other world.

"The imam has sent someone to get you," Afrah said. "He is going to take you to the Sultan."

"Oh, my goodness!" Noor felt as though she had been slapped. All this time she had been seeking the company of the Sultan, but she did not really believe that it would happen. What was she going to say? How should she act? All of a sudden, Noor was thinking to herself, 'Have I lost my mind? I am not fit to be presented to the Sultan!'

Noor washed her face and glanced at the sky. She had slept through the noon worship. That was not like her, and now she was going to see the Sultan without the benefit of having said all her prayers. 'I am such an idiot,' she thought.

"I am pleased to meet you, Great Sultan," Noor managed to utter through trembling lips. She felt so small and weak standing before the sullen man as he looked down on her from his ornate throne. His attendants stood around the Sultan. As they all stared at Noor, she felt foolish and inadequate.

"Why have you come?" the Sultan asked, wasting no time on small talk.

"I—I—well, sir, my community— it has been overcome by three evil jinn, Arrogance, Greed, and Gossip. The wealth of the silver mine has greatly improved our lives, but the people have become unkind. They are snooty and selfish. They can't trust

73

one another. Most of them have stopped coming to the *masjid for *salat. They are too busy counting their money. They are always trying to figure out wrong ways to become richer. They entertain themselves by saying bad things about innocent people."

"This is a sad situation indeed," Sultan Nabeeh replied, "but this is a concern for your imam. What do you expect me to do about it?"

"Well, I have some ideas!" Noor blurted. As soon as she said that, she wondered, 'What's wrong with me? I don't have any ideas.' She remembered the cat's whispering to her that she would have ideas at the right time. Her mind flashed an image of the strange, little man in the red robe with his broom. "You have the answers within your-self," she heard him say inside her mind. The voice of the Jew added, "The one who works for good will find happiness." The nuns visited Noor's memory. "Think of Jesus as your big brother looking out for you." Finally Noor remembered her father, Imam Yusuf, who had taught her to follow the *Sunnah of the Prophet of Allah.

"Well?" the Sultan's voice interrupted her thoughts.

Noor looked up at the Sultan. She realized he was waiting to hear her brilliant ideas. Noor straightened her shoulders and breathed a silent *BismAllah. She imagined how Prophet Muhammed (peace upon him) might have presented himself —with an aura of authority and wisdom tempered with humility. Suddenly words tumbled from Noor's mouth as if on their own. She felt inspiration coming from God, and she explained a plan to the Sultan. He listened intently to her elaborate scheme.

When Noor had finished speaking, Sultan Nabeeh stared at her silently. He rubbed his dark, gray-streaked beard. A faint smile seemed to be trying to hide itself in the sullen, mysterious face of the pensive Sultan.

Finally he responded, "I usually do not get involved in such matters, but I am impressed with your boldness and your perseverance. I will help you carry out your plans."

The Sultan looked away from Noor as if he had suddenly decided to ignore her. A courtier took Noor by the arm and indicated by a nod of his head that she should leave. He escorted her outside the room. As he returned to the Sultan's chamber, another courtier escorted Noor outside.

Noor felt awkward. "But, now what?" she asked, but the courtier said nothing. He simply left her standing there on the steps of the palace.

Noor was not sure how to get back to Raatib's and Afrah's house. As she descended the steps, someone asked, "How did your meeting go?"

Noor looked out into the street and was delighted to see Imam Nawfal. She was so relieved that she rushed over to him. She told him all about her conversation with the Sultan and her confusion about what to do next.

"Don't worry so much, my child," comforted Imam Nawfal. "Let Allah take care of the worries."

Two days passed with no word from the Sultan. Noor began to wonder if she had only imagined her meeting with him. Finally, a courtier of the palace came for her. Noor was taken to an office at the palace. A solemn woman wrote down Noor's ideas. Noor went over everything that she had told the Sultan.

"Is that it?" the all-business-like woman asked when Noor had finished talking.

"Yes, ma'am," Noor answered.

"That will be all then," the woman said as she closed her notebook and got up. She left the room, and, as if by magic, a courtier appeared to escort Noor out.

Noor felt as if she were in a boat with no oars. She had initiated the trip, but now she was going along for the ride with no control over where the trip was taking her.

Six more days passed. Raatib and Afrah assured Noor that they were happy to have her stay with them. Still, she felt that she was imposing.

Then one morning, Afrah responded to a knock at the door. There was a message for Noor. "Here is a copy of the invitations sent to your village," stated a hand-written message with no signature.

Noor read the accompanying invitation:

The Great Sultan
requests the pleasure of the company of
anyone in your household who is worthy of honor.
A fine reception will be held
in the banquet hall of the Palace of Sultan Nabeeh.
Only the most important
and refined citizens should appear.

The time and date were at the bottom. Underneath the date was an order: "All those not worthy of the Sultan's honor must report to the *masjid during this time."

'Well,' thought Noor, 'the assault against the arrogant has begun.'

Within a week before the reception for the arrogant, a courtier came for Noor. The Sultan wished to see her.

Noor stood before the Sultan. The mood seemed less formal than in her first meeting.

"Do you wish to witness the reception for the arrogant or attend the reception for the humble?" the Sultan asked.

"Please, Great Sultan," Noor replied, "recommend which I should do."

"You know that the reception at the *masjid will be very fine indeed. You know that the humble will be gratified and rewarded for their humility. Attend the reception for the arrogant so that you can see the result of your plan."

Noor made plans for her attendance at the palace reception. The Sultan and Imam Nawfal secretly made plans for a great feast in Noor's village. Imam Nawfal offered to lead *salat and deliver an encouraging *kutba at the village mosque. The village imam kindly accepted the offer. The Sultan would be dressed in ordinary clothes. He would humbly sit among the other worshipers. After worship, he would be introduced. Sultan Nabeeh would then speak. His speech would honor the humble citizens of the village. Afterwards, the royal chefs and attendants would serve a fine banquet in the mosque's fellowship center. Each good citizen would receive a silver medallion hanging from a red, blue, and gold ribbon.

The arrogant citizens, however, were in for their "rude awakening" as predicted by the Jew's proverb.

The day finally arrived. Noor wore a veil over her face so she would not be recognized. She stood at the entrance to the palace banquet hall and greeted those entering. Here they came in all their pomp and glory. They wore their finest clothes and smiled with self-satisfaction.

Before entering, each person had his or her right hand stamped with a newly designed symbol. "It is the Sultan's mark," they were told. Thinking it was a mark of honor, everyone was delighted. They were seated at long banquet tables. The centerpieces were made of weeds and thorns with no flowers. Everyone was surprised at the centerpieces, but no one said a word about them.

There was a small band, but the music was not joyous. "Isn't that a funeral march?" someone whispered.

Finally the servants brought out the royal meal. Everyone looked around and stared in shock and confusion. They were served nothing but sour pickles, flat bread with no yeast, and vinegar to drink. They were afraid of offending the royal palace, so the arrogant people choked down the horrible meal.

As the meal was ending, one of the commanders of the Sultan's royal army entered. He stood on a platform and addressed the guests. "You have come here today," he said, "to have bestowed upon you the honors you deserve. And so it is. Sultan Nabeeh is bestowing the *true* honors on the humble citizens at your community masjid. You are here to receive a reward of disgrace."

The commander had everyone's complete attention. People stared at him with their mouths dropped open.

"You wicked people," he continued, "all praises belong to Allah, *subhana wa ta'ala. He does not share them with arrogant fools who love only themselves. It is written in the Qur'an, 'Allah will give honor and multiple benefits to those who believe and perform good deeds. But with a terrible penalty He will punish those who are arrogant and disgraceful. Without Allah, they will find no protector or helper!'"[22]

Some people gasped; others stared in stunned silence.

The commander then told them, "The mark you received on your hand will stay with you as long as your arrogance. Tomorrow a notice will go out to your community. It will warn people to beware of those whose right hands carry the symbol of arrogance.

The symbol was stamped with an *indelible ink. It would not wash off but would gradually wear away. It was hoped, *insh'Allah, that, by the time the symbol had worn away, the people would have repented of their arrogance.

---

[22]Inspired by Surah 4: 173.

The people left in complete humiliation.

The commander told Noor, "The Sultan wishes for you to contact him when you are ready to proceed with the second phase of your plan."

Raatib saddled two donkeys and kindly escorted Noor back to her own village as she had requested. She returned to her room at the mosque, and she patrolled the community just to observe.

The arrogant people were humiliated. Everyone knew what the symbol on their hands meant. No matter where the arrogant people went, others noticed the symbol. Others were polite, but no one wanted to be best friends with arrogant people. Even the arrogant people did not want to be friends with each other. The shame soon made the arrogant people humble.

The evil jinni Arrogance soon departed, but Greed invited his sister Jealousy. The greedy people of the community became worse than before. Noor wrote a letter to Imam Nawfal and explained the situation. She asked him to inform the Sultan that phase two should begin soon.

Within a few weeks, announcements were distributed among the residents of Noor's community.

> The Kingdom of Sultan Nabeeh
> has scheduled a meeting
> for all those wishing to exceed their wealth.
> You will learn how to expand your treasures
> beyond your dreams.
> The Sultan's own accountant will help you
> learn to pinch pennies and use your money for yourself.
> A large investment is required of each participant.
> The more money you bring with you to invest,
> the greater can be your reward.

The time and date were included.

Noor planned her return to the Kingdom of Sultan Nebeeh.

The day of the meeting came. The greedy people carried large bags of money. They were excited as they arrived at the palace. Everyone was talking about what a wonderful chance this was for them. They were sure they would become even richer than before.

Each participant signed his or her name to the roster. One by one they entered the huge meeting room. Everyone was seated, and the meeting began. The first item on the agenda was the investments. Each citizen was given a tag on which to write his or her name. The tag was attached to each person's bag of money. The bags were then collected. Noor helped collect the large bundles of money. No one from her village recognized Noor. Over her face, she wore a veil of ivory lace studded with tiny blue flowers.

The Sultan's accountant took the bags. He loaded them onto a cart parked right there inside the conference room. The cart had the palace logo painted on its side. The greedy people were thrilled about the chance to join the Sultan's own investment plan.

Then the accountant made a shocking announcement. "Thank you so much for your kind contribution. With this money the Sultan intends to build a free hospital. The remainder will feed many hungry children."

The greedy people realized they had just given away most of their fortunes. The color drained from their faces.

The accountant continued. "You are the wealthiest and most generous of your village. The roster you signed will be used in collecting a special charity tax. Your wages will be *garnisheed for you, because Allah wishes to make things easy for you."

Color returned to the faces of the greedy, but it was the color of rage. People began shouting insults. Some of them clinched their fists and raced toward the accountant. The security guards had to rescue the nervous accountant who feared for his life.

Finally a small brigade of soldiers came in to get the people under control. Their commander addressed the greedy people. "What is wrong with you people?" he asked. "You knew what to expect when you signed into the conference."

"We were told that the money we brought would be an *investment!*" shouted a man.

"We expected to *expand* our wealth, not deplete it!" screamed a woman.

"'Treasures beyond your dreams,'" another man yelled; "—that's what the notice said."

"And the Sultan has made it easy for you to achieve such goals," the commander assured. "Your generosity will be rewarded in Heaven wherein your real treasures are kept. Those are the treasures which will never decay, the eternal treasures."

Although they felt tricked, no one could argue with the commander's words.

"It is written in the Qur'an," he continued, "'Those who donate from their resources by night and by day—secretly and publicly—have a reward with their Sovereign Lord where there will be no fear or grief. Those who charge an exorbitant amount of interest on loans will appear only as those whom the Evil One has driven to madness. They think that business requires *usury. Allah, however, permits business and forbids usury. After receiving direction from their Sovereign Lord, those who stop practicing usury will be pardoned for the past, and Allah will consider their cases. Those who continue, however, will be companions of the fire where they will abide. Allah will deprive usury of growth, but He will increase amounts given in charity. He does not show love to ungrateful, wicked characters.

"'Those who believe, perform good deeds, establish regular prayer routines, and regularly give to charities will be rewarded with their Sovereign Lord where there will be no fear or grief.

"'O believers, if you truly are believers, fear Allah and relinquish the interest amounts on accounts based on usury. If you don't, be advised of strife from Allah and His messenger, but if you repent, you may retain your principle amounts. Do not treat others unfairly, and you will not be treated unfairly.

"'If a debtor is having a difficult time, then postpone payments until he can more comfortably repay the loan. But it's better for you, if you only realized it, if, as an act of charity, you just forget the loan altogether. Fear the day when you shall be brought before Allah; then every soul shall be paid its due, and no one will be treated unjustly.'"[23]

Everyone fell silent for a while. Finally one meek voice spoke up. "But the notice said that we would be helped to pinch pennies for *our own* use."

"Yes," agreed the commander, "and when you have given most of your wealth in charity, you will indeed have been helped. You will be forced to become smart in spending in order to live on your modest income."

The commander left, and everyone at the conference was appalled at what had befallen them.

Noor went to speak with the *disheveled accountant. She managed to crack a few jokes and got him to laugh. Before she left, the accountant advised her to contact the Sultan when she was ready for the third phase of her plan.

People began giving up their acts of greed and usury. Finally the evil jinni Greed packed and got out of town. Jealousy stuck around to help Gossip. Evil people used every chance to spread rumors and invent false tales. They made fun of others and called them names.

Gossip caused a very tragic episode seriously affecting two families. A lovely, young widow had a set of three porcelain vases for sale. A teenage boy wanted to buy the vases for his mother for her birthday, but he did not have the money. The widow offered to give him the vases in return for labor. She needed a new lot and house for her chickens. The boy was happy about the deal. Two or three times a week he would go to the widow's house. He worked on building the chicken house and putting wire around the lot. Some busybodies noticed the boy's coming to and going from the widow's house. They started a rumor that the boy and widow were doing something wrong. The rumor was a lie. The boy and the widow had always acted properly. The rumor quickly spread among the students at the boy's school. The boy told the truth, but his classmates did not believe him. They said mean things to him. A click of students began

---

[23]Inspired by Surah 2: 274-281.

sneaking hateful messages inside the boy's books. Cruel graffiti was scrawled on the outside walls of the widow's home. The widow felt that her reputation was ruined and that she could no longer live there. The widow moved many miles away. Her moving increased the gossip, however. The teenage boy became very upset. He finally killed himself by thrusting his body onto a doubled-edged sword. The boy's entire family, of course, felt terrible. His mother was even more saddened when she learned the whole story of how he was working to earn the vases for her birthday. The mother cried so much that she finally had to get counseling at a clinic.

Noor sought company with the Sultan. He was greatly grieved by the bad news. "I admit that I was not convinced at first," he said to Noor. "I wasn't sure that your community's problems were really as grave as you had described them to me. The news about the boy and the widow proves that your concerns did need attention."

Phase three of Noor's plan was initiated. A message from the Palace of the Sultan was sent to everyone in Noor's village.

Although the recent suicide of the young student
was quite unfortunate,
those who brought the improper affair to light
must be recognized.
The Kingdom of Sultan Nabeeh

is thankful to have the royal domain advised
of such sin in order to suppress it.
All persons involved in letting the affair be known
are invited to a royal meal and *salat service in honor of
the innocent people hurt by recent events.
If you are among those to be thanked
for informing society of the affair,
the Sultan requests your presence
in the palace banquet hall.

The date and time were noted.

All those who had been involved in the gossip were delighted. They were happy that the Sultan was recognizing their efforts. The nasty click of students and other awful people accepted the Sultan's invitation. 'What a wonderful idea,' they thought. 'The Sultan is going to honor people just for sharing stories about terrible people.'

The gossipers had heard of the previous banquet for the arrogant. They were happy to see beautiful flowers on the table. They smelled the tempting fragrance of good food and were relieved. The servants attended to the guests. Each guest was served a hefty portion of shredded, pink meat. No one was sure what it was, but the meat was delicious and sweet. There was nothing else to eat, however. There was such a huge amount on each plate that no one wanted to finish it all. Hiding her face with a veil, Noor started a rumor. She said that anytime a guest did not finish all his or her food, the Sultan became very offended. She claimed that he had banished people from the kingdom and had even had guests' heads chopped off. The guests were afraid not to finish all their meat. They gorged themselves to the point of being sick.

Finally the Sultan made a grand entrance, and the people applauded. The Sultan welcomed the guests. Noor said to him, "Great Sultan, your guests have enjoyed this great feast, and they have asked what it is. They have never tasted meat so sweet and delicious."

"Summon the chef," the Sultan said to one of his attendants. "We shall soon discover what this wonderful dish is that he has prepared just for you, my honored guests."

The chef appeared, and the Sultan asked him to reveal his secret. "Oh, Great Sultan," the chef explained, "this is the flesh of the young man who killed himself because of the vile words of the gossipers. It is the flesh of all those injured by the gossipers' lies and vicious rumors."

The people were horrified. They didn't know that the meal was really an unusual dish of ostrich meat. It was seasoned with a sweet sauce made of crushed tomatoes (hence the pink color), apple cider vinegar, brown sugar, honey, and spices.

"You wicked, horrible people," the Sultan said. "Do you think I invited you here to be honored for your careless, sinful words? You should be ashamed of your evil deeds! Have you not read the Qur'an?: 'O believers, do not allow any of the men among you to laugh at others. It may be that those ridiculed are better than such men. Do not allow any of the women to laugh at others. It may be that those ridiculed are better than such women. Do not defame or be sarcastic to one another. Do not call each other ugly names. An unflattering name that means something evil is fitting for a believer who trespasses in such a manner. Those who continue are in the wrong.

"'O believers, avoid being overly suspicious because some suspicions are sinful. Do not spy on each other, and do not gossip. Would you eat the flesh of your dead brother? No, you would abhor it! But fear Allah who is the Most Forgiving, the Most Merciful.'[24]

"Gossip," the Sultan continued, "destroys a person by ruining his or her reputation. The enjoyment of gossip is like *cannibalism. Go home, you evil people, before I have your heads chopped off! Prostrate before Allah, confess your evil deeds, and beg for His forgiveness."

The banquet hall was hurriedly vacated.

The Sultan sat down with Noor. "What are your plans now, my dear? Are you returning home?"

Noor removed her veil. "I have no home, my dear Sultan," Noor said, daring to return his affectionate term of address.

"You are very wise for your age, and I have need of good counsel. There are many rooms in this palace. Stay as one of my advisors," the Sultan invited.

"Oh, Great Sultan," Noor said with amazement, "I am not worthy of such honor. I am a child and a simple person. I have no wisdom to share with the Great Sultan."

---

[24]Inspired by Surah 49: 11-12.

"Shall I have your head chopped off then?" the Sultan teased as a faint smile flickered.

Noor was surprised to see the humorous side of Sultan Nabeeh.

A servant brought tea and set the table for two. Noor and the Sultan were served a pleasant dinner of colorful vegetables, stir-fried in olive oil and sprinkled with an assortment of spices.

Sultan Nabeeh motioned for an attendant. "Have a room prepared for the young lady," the Sultan ordered. "She will be staying for quite a while."

Adventures of the Palace

Shown above is the palace logo of the Kingdom of Sultan Nabeeh. The lamp is a symbol of all knowledge and wisdom, which belong to God. The star shooting from the flame represents God's gift of knowledge and wisdom to anyone who seeks truth. The olive branch is symbolic of the peace that comes from being a devoted servant of God. The crescent moon is a design used in both Islam and Judaism in connection with new moon festivals and calendars based on the moon. When we see the crescent moon, we may be reminded that what a person knows of God is only a small measure. Just as the moon becomes fuller in stages, a person understands more of God as he or she matures in the spiritual life. There is also a mysterious, dark side of the moon. In the same way, there will always be divine mysteries known only to God. Red, green, and blue are the primary colors of light. On the ribbon these three colors are symbolic of the body, mind, and soul of each person. When someone submits his or her whole self to God, all three aspects of being must be devoted to God. A servant must safeguard his or her body (for example, no cigarettes or drugs). A servant is careful of what he or she puts into his or her mind (for example, no vulgar music or magazines). A servant is devoted to doing what is best for his or her soul (for example, taking time to pray and study Scriptures).

God promises, "...Certainly I will never allow the accomplishments of anyone—male or female—to be for loss. You are each a part of the whole group..." (inspired by Surah 3: 195). Life is a journey, and sometimes its twists and turns are unpredictable, and the journey seems uncertain. God, however, is in our future as well as in our past and present. He is always before us preparing the way. People who devote their lives to serving God (blessed and exalted is He!) can be assured of His constant presence and guidance. God uses his servants—male and female—in every area of society. Sometimes He has wonderful surprises for us in the great adventure of life.

Arabic words to learn:
mufassir (moo-fas-seer) plural: mufassireen. A person who interprets the meanings of the Qur'an.
saba' al'kheer (sa-ba al-kheer) <u>Morning of goodness</u>; used as "good morning."
saba' anoor (sa-ba a-noor) <u>Morning of light</u>; used as "good morning."
salAllahu alahe wa salam (sa-la-hoo a-la-he wa sa-lam) <u>May the peace and blessings of God be upon him</u>.

The blessing spoken or written after the name of Prophet Muhammed.

Sharia (sha-ree-a) Islamic law based on the *Qur'an and on the *Hadith and *Sunnah of Prophet Muhammed.

The Sultan's wife *Amani happily received Noor into the palace household. The *Sultan and *Sultana had three wonderful sons, but their only daughter had died as a baby. Noor's delightful presence helped to finally heal the pain left by the baby girl's death. Amani gave Noor all the attention that Amani had missed giving her own daughter. Noor gained the mother image she never before had. Everyone was happier.

Months later, Sultan *Nabeeh became unusually pensive even for him. He seemed heavily burdened. Sometimes he was unaware of conversations around him. Whisper, the *jinni cat, discovered the Sultan's secret burden. One morning the Sultan prayed alone in his private chamber, and Whisper overheard. The Sultan asked for God's guidance. The Sultan had to choose which one of the three princes should succeed him as the Great Sultan. It was a decision not to be made carelessly. The easy choice would have been simply to choose the oldest. Sultan Nabeeh wanted to make the best choice, not the easiest.

Whisper had an idea. While the Sultan slept, the cat whispered into his ear, "Ask each son which animal is his favorite." Whisper thought that at least one son would vote for the amazing cat. The son choosing the cat would certainly make the best Sultan.

When Sultan Nabeeh awoke, he remembered the idea. He thought it seemed a rather strange way of choosing a sultan. He had learned to trust his dreams, however, and he thought that he had dreamed the idea. He decided to bring it up at brunch.

Noor sat with the Sultan, the Sultana, and the sons at the table. The youngest son *Masoud was about Noor's age. The oldest, *Labeeb was about five years older. The middle son *Hamsa was two years older than Noor.

The servant began pouring tea into the cups. Amani passed a dish of date-stuffed pastries to Noor.

Feeling a bit foolish, Sultan Nabeeh said, "Well, I've been thinking of adopting a palace mascot and would like you boys' opinion about which animal to choose."

Everyone stared at the Sultan as if they were wondering, 'From where did that come?' No one had ever mentioned anything about a mascot before. It seemed a bit out of character for the serious Sultan.

Whisper the cat jumped into Noor's lap. Whisper peered over the top of the table and looked at the boys. "Cat!" she whispered. "The cat."

Finally Labeeb spoke up. "The dog. The dog is a loyal, obedient companion, and it can be trained to attack."

Masoud jeered, "Surely we can come up with something more original that a goofy dog. How about the monkey? Monkeys are entertaining, funny, and playful."

"No; no," Whisper yelled as loud as a whisper can get. "The cat!"

"Monkeys don't even live around here, you clown," Labeeb said with a laugh.

"Yeah, you clown," whispered Whisper.

"I know it's not original," said Hamsa, "and maybe it's too obvious, but I can't think of any animal better for our mascot than the camel. Camels serve our people every day. To all Muslims, the camel is a symbol of strength and honor."

"Wait a minute; hold everything," Masoud announced. "Before we make a firm decision, I have one question. Which one of us is going to have to share his bed with this mascot?"

Everyone laughed at that.

The boys hurried off to various classes and activities.

The Sultan, Amani, and Noor sat quietly for a minute. Amani just stared at Sultan Nabeeh. Finally, she couldn't keep quiet any longer. "Are you really going to—?"

"No," he abruptly interrupted. "I don't know why I—well, yes, I do." The Sultan released a big sigh. "I need to decide which of our sons should be the next Sultan. Somehow I got the silly notion that I could make a decision by asking them to choose an animal."

'Silly?' thought Whisper who had sulked to the corner for her bowl of milk.

"It's not too silly," said Amani. "I think the conversation was quite revealing. Labeeb suggested the dog because of its obedience to serve and to attack on command. Perhaps that suggests that he would surround himself with people who pamper him and are too quick to go to war. Masoud preferred the monkey. Does that mean he would spend his time monkeying around on the throne? Hamsa pointed out the qualities of the camel. Leaders should have those same qualities, shouldn't they?"

"I finally remember why I married you," the Sultan teased. "I hope the new Sultan will find a wife with as much wisdom as mine." He glanced at Noor thoughtfully. "Still, I can't base my decision on what's happening at the zoo," he said rather flippantly.

The servant refilled Amani's teacup.

"You need to spend more time with your sons. Learn how they each think, feel, and perceive," said Amani.

Noor had been silent throughout this family conversation. She finally suggested, "Perhaps they could serve as your advisors for a time. That way you could see just how they would perform as leaders."

"Of course that makes the most sense," agreed the Sultan. "For one thing, I'm not sleeping with a camel in *my* bed." Noor and Amani laughed, and the Sultan felt relieved that he had discussed his burden with his two favorite gals.

It was the custom of the Sultan to spend one morning each week listening to appeals. Sometimes convicts felt that they were unfairly convicted. They came to ask the Sultan to consider their cases. Victims also came forward to complain when they felt that justice had not been served. The Sultan's legal advisors reviewed each case. If the advisors approved, a case could be presented before the Sultan. Sultan Nabeeh decided that the appeals court would be a good way to observe his sons as they made decisions.

The youngest son Masoud sat in the chair nearest Sultan Nabeeh. Several people—victims and convicts—presented new evidence. With the Sultan's supervision, Masoud decided what course of action should be taken concerning each case. Sometimes a court decision was either changed or confirmed; other times a new trial was ordered.

Making fair decisions was not difficult when the evidence was clear and obvious, but then an angry man appeared who had no evidence. He simply wanted something done about his situation.

"I have made my report to the police," the victim complained. "They have done nothing to recover my stolen goods."

"Okay," Masoud coaxed. "Just explain exactly what happened."

"I had traveled far to obtain some excellent *alabaster windows for my house. The night became very dark as I neared the city. I still had some distance to go and was tired. I decided to sleep before traveling the remaining distance. When I awoke, the windows were gone—cart and all. I must have been sleeping like a rock; I didn't hear a thing. I paid a great sum of money for those alabaster windows, and I expect the police to recover them!"

"Do you have any idea at all who might have taken them?" Masoud asked.

"No. It's the police department's job to investigate!"

"If there were no witnesses, and you have no evidence, there's little the police can do to find the thieves," responded Masoud. The Sultan listened intently but did not interrupt.

"Listen!" the man spoke much more boldly to young Masoud than he would ever have dared to speak to the Sultan. "I've lived in this city all my life, and I've paid taxes all my life! I demand that something be done!"

"Well," Masoud said, "was there anyone else around who might have seen something?"

"No one but the tree where I slept," quipped the man, a bit haughtily.

"Okay, then!" decided Masoud. "We'll arrest the tree as our first suspect."

Sultan Nabeeh turned to look at Masoud.

"I didn't come here to listen to some kid's jokes!" the man said angrily.

Sultan Nabeeh was about to have the man removed because of his disrespect, but Masoud continued the conversation.

"I'm not joking." Masoud addressed an officer of the court, "Officer, I want you to send some police out and have the tree chained and questioned."

Sultan Nabeeh leaned toward his son and asked in a low voice, "What kind of monkeying around is this?"

Masoud leaned toward his father and said, "I have an idea, Father. Let me carry it through."

The Sultan was not convinced. "You'll make a laughing stock of the palace."

92

"If my idea doesn't work, Father, you can blame it on your idiot son."

"But I don't want my son to be an idiot."

"Please, Father, give me some room here," Masoud begged.

Sultan Nabeeh studied for a minute, rubbed his beard, and then motioned for the officer to do as Masoud had ordered. 'After all,' thought the Sultan, 'sooner or later I have to allow my sons the freedom to be idiots if that's what they want.'

The victim huffed. Grumbling mumbled comments, he led the police to the tree underneath which he had slept when the crime occurred. The police felt like clowns when they wrapped the tree in chains and began questioning it in vain. People gathered around and laughed when they saw what was going on.

"That tree must have an awfully ferocious *bark* to get arrested," someone joked.

"Yeah, but if it were a *dog*wood tree, its bite would be worse than its bark," joked someone else.

Another joker said, "That's one way to get to the *root* of the problem."

"Talk about going out on a *limb*," someone added.

The whole thing became a big joke around the city. As Masoud had hoped, the joking became so ordinary that the thieves started talking loosely. Someone reported their suspicious bragging, and the police obtained a search warrant. The alabaster windows were discovered behind one braggart's home. The windows were still loaded on the cart and covered with a large rug. Three teenage boys were apprehended, and each one accused the other two for making him "go along with it."

The Sultan was amazed at how well his son's scheme had worked. It had seemed so stupid, but really it was quite clever.

Being the oldest, Labeeb was a bit disgruntled that his youngest brother got to serve on the appeals court first. The Sultan simply said, "Ooops," and arranged for Labeeb to have his turn next.

Immediately before the appeals court began, one of the Sultan's advisors came in with a report. A man-eating lion had been terrorizing some nearby villages. Two people had been killed, and three others had escaped with serious injuries. The advisor suggested that a special task force be assembled. The Sultan had to consider that matter in addition to the appeals.

Labeeb handled case after case in a thoughtful and fair manner. The last person to appear before the throne was a woman representing her husband. She claimed that her husband had been arrested on false charges.

"It was all a big misunderstanding," she explained. "My husband wants to be brave and respected, but he's really a wimp. He went around bragging how many of his enemies he had killed. He let everyone think that he was talking about people. He had really only killed 583 flies."

"Flies?" Labeeb asked. "You mean as in 'buzz buzz'?"

"Yes, bugs," she clarified. "He wanted people to think he was really tough. He would not even testify at his own trial that he had killed flies, not people."

Labeeb chuckled while Sultan Nabeeh kept his usual stern face.

Labeeb turned to the advisor who had reviewed the case. "Was any evidence presented to indicate that this man had killed anyone—uh, human, I mean?"

The advisor replied, "There were several witnesses, but their only testimony was the suspect's own bragging. Some bones were dug up in the suspect's back yard, but they turned out not to be human."

"That was a wild boar that kept digging up my flowers. I knocked it in the head with a shovel and killed it myself," boasted the woman.

"There have not even been any recent reports of missing persons," added the advisor.

"Alright," Labeeb began stating his decision. "Your husband is to go free, but I have an order for him."

With a questioning look, Sultan Nabeeh turned to his son.

"By order of the Court of Sultan Nebeeh," Labeeb commanded, "your husband — uh, what's his name?"

"*Usamah," informed the advisor.

"Usamah," continued Labeeb, "is hereby commanded to hunt down the man-eating lion which has been attacking local villagers."

The woman stood there with her mouth hanging open. Her husband was a complete coward. How could he possibly hunt down a lion? Still, she could not argue with the court, especially after asking for Usamah's freedom.

The court recorder documented the command and gave the woman a copy for her husband.

"Well, that was unusual," commented Sultan Nebeeh, "but whatever works."

"I thought perhaps the man would find his courage," explained Labeeb with a smile.

Usamah's wife delivered his release papers and presented him the order to hunt the lion. Usamah begged the prison guard to let him stay locked up. The police had to drag Usamah out of jail. As they were trying to throw him outside, he grabbed hold of the doorframe. When Usamah was finally jerked away, a piece of the doorframe broke off and was still in his hands. Usamah cried all the way home as his wife led him by the hand.

The next morning, Usamah's wife packed some supplies and saddled the donkey. She shoved a sword in Usamah's hand, pushed him outside, and locked the door. "Don't come home without that lion!" she yelled through the door.

Usamah rode around in circles all day. He avoided the area near the villages that had been attacked. He chased lizards, threw rocks at rabbits, traded songs with the birds, and drew pictures in the sand, but he did not try to find the *renegade lion.

Finally it became dark. Usamah was afraid of the dark, and he was afraid of man-eating beasts that roamed in the dark. He finally trembled himself to sleep.

Usamah was sleeping soundly when the man-eating lion came prowling about. The donkey, tied to a bush, was frightened by the lion. The donkey jerked itself free and ran away. The lion, however, was not interested in the donkey. It smelled the sweaty hide of a human. But it smelled something else too. The *alfalfa that Usamah's wife had packed for the donkey was not weed-free. A plant that causes sleepiness had been mixed up with the alfalfa. Out of curiosity, the lion stuck its nose into the donkey's feedbag. A feeling of calm came over the lion, and it lay down to continue sniffing the plant. The lion became drowsy and fell asleep with its nose in the feedbag.

The next morning when Usamah awoke, he became terrified. The lion was lying just a few feet from him. Usamah saw that the lion did not move and wondered if it was dead. Usamah got up the nerve to get a closer look. The lion was breathing and appeared to be unconscious. Usamah wanted to run away, but the donkey was gone. Usamah thought that if he ran on foot, the lion might smell him when it woke up. The lion could then find Usamah by tracking his scent. Usamah picked a stick off the

96

ground, climbed a nearby tree, and poked the lion with the stick. It didn't move; it was completely unaware—in a deep, deep sleep.

Usamah climbed down and got the rope his wife had packed. He nervously tied the lion's mouth shut and tied its legs together. Usamah removed the feedbag. After a few minutes, the lion began to stir. Usamah realized that something in the alfalfa had made the lion sleepy. Usamah tied the feedbag over the lion's nose. Then he went to look for the donkey. Fortunately, the donkey had not gone far, and it was looking for Usamah as well. Usamah struggled to get the docile lion onto the donkey's back. The lion was heavy, and the donkey was nervous. The donkey did not think that having a lion on its back was a good idea. Usamah and the donkey seemed to be dancing in circles. Usamah finally succeeded, and then he headed for home.

Usamah's wife was digging in her flower garden. She looked up to see her cowardly husband coming home with the renegade lion. She nearly fainted from surprise. "You're a hero!" she exclaimed. "Tell me all about your adventure."

"Oh, there's not much to tell," Usamah said casually. "The lion was terrified when he saw me charging after him with my sword. He ran, but I pursued him, wrestled him down, and tied him up."

"Why is he so calm?" asked the wife, curiously staring at the lion.

"Oh, he—he fainted from fear."

"And why did you tie the donkey's feed bag to the lion?"

"Oh, well—uh—uh," Usamah struggled for an answer. "I'm teaching him what to eat after I've—uh—removed his teeth."

"You're going to remove his teeth?"

"Yes—uh—and his claws too," replied Usamah as he invented his tale. "Do you have any more of that alfalfa?"

Usamah was scared silly. He gave the lion a fresh batch of alfalfa to snort. Then Usamah got a pair of pliers and began pulling out the lion's claws. Usamah's brow dripped sweat as, one by one, he removed each claw and put it in a small pouch. "Well, that went okay," he said as he put the last claw in the pouch."

"Now for the teeth," his wife said.

"I sure am hungry," Usamah said. "Could you go ahead and take out the teeth while I grab a bite to eat?"

"And rob you of some of the glory? Absolutely not," the wife answered.

"No, really; it's okay," Usamah insisted. "I don't mind."

"Oh, no; I'm just happy that you're happy. I'll go fix you something to eat while you finish the job."

"No! No!" Usamah exclaimed. "Stay here; don't leave me. I mean—uh—I—I need you to hold the pouch."

"Well, okay," said the wife.

Usamah loosened the rope from around the lion's nose. He held his hands to Heaven and breathed a prayer. Finally he started pulling. "Uhhhh! This is hard," said Usamah.

"You can do it!" the wife encouraged.

"Uhhhhh!" he grunted. Finally all the teeth were pulled. Relieved, Usamah sat down and cried like a baby. "Oh, I'm just happy; these are tears of joy," Usamah lied.

Usamah removed the food bag. He put a bridle on the drowsy, toothless, clawless, man-eating, alfalfa-sniffing lion, and led it into the city. At first, everyone stared in disbelief, but then people cheered and gathered around Usamah. They patted him on the back and praised him. News quickly reached the palace that Usamah was bringing in the *renegade lion.

Usamah appeared before the throne and presented the Sultan with the pouch of teeth and claws. Usamah explained, "I wrestled this man-eating lion and caught him with my bare hands. I pulled out his teeth and claws and taught him to eat alfalfa."

Sultan Nabeeh was almost speechless. "And you're the same man who brags about killing *flies*?"

"Well," replied Usamah, "I just hate to brag about my *real* adventures. I don't want to put everyone else to shame."

The lion was donated to a nature club trying to establish a petting zoo. Usamah was awarded a hero's medal of honor and a sum of reward money. He and his proud wife went on a second honeymoon—somewhere far away from lions and other such beasties.

Sultan Nabeeh had been quite impressed with his youngest and oldest sons. Now it was Hamsa's turn. Hamsa listened to each case and determined what course of action to take. He kept the same sullen expression as his father. His manner demanded respect as it gave him the appearance of strength and wisdom.

The case of the stolen alabaster windows had been solved earlier. Two young thieves had been ordered to serve jail time. The oldest thief had been condemned to have both his hands cut off. The parents of the oldest thief now appeared before the court. The parents were pleading that their sons' hands not be cut off.

Hamsa turned to the advisor who had reviewed the case. "Why have two criminals been given a light sentence, and this third, the severe punishment of having his hands cut off?"

"This was the first crime of the two younger thieves," the advisor explained, "but the oldest boy has a long criminal history. Also, it is believed that he urged the two young teens to assist him in the theft."

"It is written in the Qur'an," Hamsa proclaimed to the parents, "'As for the thief— male or female—cut off his or her hands as an example and a punishment from Allah on account of the crime. Allah is Exalted in Power and Wisdom. But if the thief repents after his or her crime and amends his or her conduct, Allah responds with forgiveness. Allah is the Most Forgiving and the Most Merciful.'[25]

"How many times has the young man been convicted of stealing?" Hamsa asked the advisor.

"He has been charged seven times," reported the advisor, "and seven times he repented and was pardoned. He has not amended his conduct as the Qur'an says he should. The court found that the young man had made no attempts to improve his life. He has not changed his bad behavior. The court decided that he would never stop stealing until his hands were cut off as dictated by the Qur'an."

"Please, kind sir," begged the criminal's mother. "Despite his failures, he is our son and we love him." She began to cry.

Her husband continued. "Please find it in your heart to give him this one last chance. We will do everything within our power to cause our son to abandon his evil lifestyle and follow the Straight Way."

---

[25]Inspired by Surah 5: 38-39.

"But if he hasn't changed after seven chances already—," Hamsa began. But he had pity on the parents. Hamsa turned to his father. "Father, if a person's hands are cut off, and then he or she repents, how can Allah then show mercy? The person's hands cannot be put back on."

"The mercy is in the forgiveness," replied the Sultan.

"But, Father," Hamsa said, "the Scripture says that Allah is the Most Forgiving *AND* the Most Merciful. If the mercy is only in the forgiveness, why would the Scripture add a separate title concerning mercy?"

The Sultan understood Hamsa's point.

Hamsa pondered for a few seconds, and then asked, "Father, is there anything in the *Sharia that says exactly how the hands should be cut off?"

"No," the Sultan answered. "In fact the legal advisors do not agree about when this verse should apply. They wonder what should be the value of the stolen merchandise before such severe punishment is done. And they wonder when only one hand should be cut off. You must ask yourself, is alabaster worth a man's hands? And you must determine, if the young man is given another chance, will his next crime involve murder? It's a huge decision."

"If there is nothing in the Sharia specifying the exact method of how the hands should be cut off, then I am ready to make my decision," Hamsa told his father.

"Very well," the Sultan agreed.

Hamsa poised himself and announced his decision. "I am sorry for the grief your son has caused you," he said to the distraught parents. "It is his actions that have resulted in your grief, not the actions of the court. The Kingdom of Sultan Nabeeh abides by the laws of the Qur'an and Sunnah. These laws are quite clear. Anyone who breaks a law is responsible for his or her own actions. He or she must face the penalty. It is my decision to uphold the court's decision to cut off the hands of the unrepentant thief."

"Oh, no, no," the mother wailed.

"But not by *amputation," Hamsa continued.

Everyone fell silent as they listened for Hamsa's explanation.

"The hands of this thief shall be cut off from doing anything for his own benefit. From this day forward, his hands shall belong to the Kingdom of the Sultan Nabeeh.

The Word of your Lord
is fulfilled
through truth and justice'.
Nothing can change
His words.
He is the All-Hearing
All-Knowing One.

inspired by
Surah 6: 115

His legs will be put into chains, and his hands shall perform labor in the service of the public. He shall be housed, clothed, and fed by the prison system, but he will receive no money or other payment for his work. He shall perform deeds that will benefit the citizens of the kingdom. He will work in such areas as road work, public parks and gardens, and trash pick-up. This work will last for the rest of his life—or until the convict shows that he is sorry and wants to change. Then he can be granted the privilege of appearing before this court of appeals."

This day became known as one of the rare occasions in which Sultan Nabeeh smiled from his throne. "My son is a *mufassir," he proudly said.

Hamsa's decision set a *precedent. After his idea, a community-service, work-release program was designed. It became so effective that other sultans sent people to study the program. The plan was then used in other kingdoms.

That evening, Sultan Nabeeh was unusually quiet and absorbed in his thoughts.

"What is so heavy on your mind, my dear, dear Nabeeh?" Amani asked.

"I am no closer to choosing the next Sultan than I was a month ago," replied the Sultan. "I am equally proud of all my sons. How can I choose one?"

"Wisdom will guide you in her own time, Nabeeh," Amani comforted.

"I know," he said, "but could you give me a little hint?"

She laughed at his vague humor.

Days later, the royal family with its *entourage paraded down main street. They were going to the grand opening of the new, free hospital. People waited along the store-fronts and street markets. They waved, cheered, and threw kisses for the royal family.

A street sign had loosened from its bolts during a recent windstorm. It chose this time to come toppling down. It fell right on the hind end of a horse. The horse broke loose from its owner's hold on the reins. It galloped at high speed up the street toward the royal family. The alarming shrieks of the people further excited the horse. As fate would have it, there was a very old man, deaf and unaware of what was happening. The old man stepped right into the path of the runaway horse.

Masoud ran toward the horse, waved his hands, and shouted, "Stop! Stop!"

Labeeb ran for
the horse, grabbed its reins,
and tried to pull the frenzied,
speeding horse to a stop.

Hamsa ran for the old man. He shoved his
own body upon the unsuspecting gentleman. He propelled himself and the old man out
of the way of the horse. Hamsa had learned in self-defense class how to tuck-and-roll
when falling. He was able to hold onto the old man and keep him and himself from
getting hurt.

The crowd loved it. They cheered as if it had all happened for their entertainment
pleasure.

Sultan Nabeeh observed the entire incident. He stood still and quiet for a moment, and then told his wife, "I've just made my decision."

The Sultan would later explain to her, "Masoud acted as if his orders alone should make things happen in an emergency. Labeeb thinks he's a super hero; he tried to stop an excited, galloping horse. Hamsa did not waste any time. He put himself in harm's way to rescue one of the common citizens. He showed quick, clear thinking. He has the attitude of serving the people. Those things are necessary for the office of the Sultan."

Amani would agree that he had made the wisest choice.

Next came an even more difficult chore. Sultan Nabeeh had to tell his sons which one was chosen. Sultan Nabeeh called his sons and his wife into his private chamber.

"I asked you boys to serve beside me on the appeals court for a reason," Sultan Nabeeh began. "Your actions helped guide me in making a difficult decision. I had to choose which one of you should be my successor. I was very proud of all of you. It seemed an impossible task to choose just one of you for such an honor. At long last, however, I have made my decision. *Insh'Allah, Hamsa will be the next Sultan of the Kingdom of Sultan Nabeeh."

Hamsa was pleased, but he acted calmly and did not cheer for himself. He did not want to seem arrogant.

Labeeb heaved a sigh and sunk his face into his open palms.

Sultan Nabeeh put his hand on Labeeb's shoulder to comfort him. "Please do not feel that this is a rejection, my son. You have many wonderful qualities, and I—"

"Oh, no, Father," Labeeb interrupted. "I'm not grieving; I'm thanking Allah, *subhana wa ta-ala."

"What?" The Sultan was confused.

"I was so afraid you would choose me just because I'm the oldest, and I already have other plans."

"Other plans? What other plans?" The Sultan was surprised.

"I'm joining the army, Father. I want to be a commander."

"I'm glad too, Father," Masoud added. "I mean I was willing to be the Sultan if that's what you wanted, but I really want to do something else."

"Like what?" asked the astonished Sultan.

"Like go to medical school. I want to be a nurse."

"A nurse?! A nurse?!" the Sultan echoed. "Why not a doctor?"

"Well, I thought about becoming a doctor," Masoud answered, "but doctors are too busy. They can't spend much time with each patient. They figure out why people are sick, and they prescribe medicines. They tell the patients what to do to get better. But nurses are the ones who really take care of people. And that's what I want to do."

The Sultan leaned back in his chair and was speechless. It had never occurred to him that any of his sons would not want to follow in his footsteps. He realized that he had been needlessly torturing himself all this time when all he really had to do was say, 'Who wants to be Sultan? You? Okay.'

Amani just sat back on the couch and smiled.

As the Sultan looked at her, a strange realization came over him. "You knew," he said to Amani. "You knew all along, didn't you? Why didn't you tell me?"

"My dear, dear Nabeeh," she said, "you had to know for yourself that the next Sultan was the best choice."

"Sometimes you're better for me than I can stand," the Sultan quipped.

"Father," Hamsa began, "could we keep this a secret—I mean about my becoming the Sultan—could we keep it a secret for awhile?"

"Certainly," said the Sultan. "Agreed?" he said as he glanced at the other two boys.

"Sure. Yeah," they said.

"Are we done here, Father?" Masoud asked. "We're supposed to go over to the hospital and help decorate the children's ward."

"Yes, go on and get out of here," the Sultan ordered, "and see if they have any headache medicine down at that hospital. I need about a case."

Masoud and Labeeb laughed and hurried out, but Hamsa lingered.

"What is it, son," Sultan Nabeeh asked.

"There is another matter I'd like to discuss," Hamsa began.

"Alright; *maybe* I can handle it," the Sultan said with dry humor.

"It's about Noor," said Hamsa. "I love her. I want to marry her."

"Well, that's up to Noor, but I have to tell you, Hamsa, that Masoud and Labeeb have also expressed the same interest."

"Yeah, that's what I figured," said Hamsa somewhat sadly. "I didn't want the fact that, insh'Allah, I will become Sultan to influence her decision."

"Well, if it did, she would probably *decline* your offer of marriage. She would think that she's not good enough to be a sultana, but she would be wrong. Aside from your mother here, Noor is the wisest, most gracious lady I've ever known."

Hamsa sat quietly.

"We will speak to Noor," Amani said as she patted her son's hand.

The Sultan took a few days to recover from all the surprises. Finally, he and Amani invited Noor to the Sultan's private chamber. Small cakes filled with nuts, raisins, and dates were served with jasmine tea. Then the servants were excused.

"Which one of my sons are you going to marry?" the Sultan asked abruptly.

Noor was stunned. "I—I—I...."

"For goodness' sake, Nabeeh!" Amani chastised. "Don't scare the poor child to death. You make it sound as if she has no choice but to marry one of our sons."

Amani took Noor's hand. "Perhaps you're interested in someone else?"

"No—uh—no," Noor stumbled.

"Of course she wants to marry one of my sons." The Sultan attempted to lighten the mood. "Where else can she find a man almost as good looking and charming as me? It's just unfortunate that none of my sons has this big, wonderful nose, but Allah only had a few like this to go around."

Amani picked up the tray of cakes and offered it to the Sultan. "Shove something into your face so Noor can have a minute to think without your nonsense."

Noor relaxed a bit and managed a smile. When the Sultan and Sultana were alone together like this, they acted like any ordinary couple. It was a side of the royal family that few people ever had the opportunity to glimpse.

"All your sons are attractive and honorable." Noor finally found some words. "I have never thought that I could marry one of them. I'm sure Masoud, Hamsa, and Labeeb know many girls who are much smarter and prettier than I."

"Actually, each of our sons has asked for your hand in marriage," Amani announced.

Noor stared into Amani's face and tried to determine if she were joking.

"It's your choice. Take your time and think about it. You can say no to all of them. They'll get over it, and we won't be offended. Of course, we'd be thrilled to have you as our daughter-in-law, but we'll always love you no matter what you decide."

Sultan Nabeeh nodded in agreement.

"But aren't you forgetting something?" Noor said. "I'm not royalty."

"Well, I have a little bit of authority around here," said the Sultan. "You are hereby declared royalty. So there; it's official."

Sometimes Noor didn't know quite what to make of the Sultan. She tried to imagine him as an old man—odd and stubborn. The image she got was just too funny.

That night Noor lay in bed in her palace room. She stared at the stars through an oval window. She thought about how her life had taken her from being an abandoned baby to belonging to the royal household. And now she was invited to take her pick of the three most amazing young men within the royal domain, the Sultan's own sons. The choice seemed too big for her.

"Which one of the Sultan's sons do you think I should marry, Whisper?" Noor asked the cat curled next to her.

"Pzzzzhh," spat the cat. "Leave me out of this one."

Noor thought about the boys. Masoud was delightful. He was always cheerful and encouraging. Noor enjoyed being around him. Hamsa was more serious, but he had his father's odd humor. Noor found comfort in that. Labeeb seemed able to tackle anything. He was strong and determined. All three were honest and honorable in every way. Noor tossed and turned all night. She wished that the Sultan had just made the decision for her.

Inspiration often comes very early in the morning. Just before dawn, Noor got an idea. She made a plan to help her choose one of the three young men. She knew she needed someone who liked her free and creative spirit. She was a casual person who could think for herself. She needed someone who allowed her to have her own space. After the morning worship, Noor sat down and wrote a poem with a secret meaning:

In bondage I am free;
  I am branded for the sake of liberty.
    Without my chains
      The threat of prison upon me gains.
        My spirit takes flight
          In tethered darkness and daylight.
            In awesome dread
              These bindings I dare not shed.
                Every day I vow to seek
                  The ties that bind my wandering feet.

Noor intended to share her unsigned poem with the boys. She hoped one of them could tell her the meaning of the poem. That one, she thought, would be the most suitable for her. She wanted someone who understood her thinking. She realized that she found peculiar ways to express herself. Could anyone appreciate that? She needed someone of a kindred spirit.

Masoud was about to start out the door when Noor caught up with him. "Masoud," she called.

He whirled around and gave her a big smile. "Noor, how is the light of my life?"

'That's what I love about him,' Noor thought. 'He always makes me feel so good.'

"Do you have a minute?" she asked.

"I always have time for you, sweet girl," he said energetically.

"I came across this poem," Noor fibbed a little. "I wondered if you could tell me what it means."

Masoud quickly read the poem. "Did that crazy cat write this? It sounds like something the cat would write. I don't know what it means. Ask Mom. She gets into weird stuff like this. Sorry. Anything else I can do for you? Like give you the moon and stars, for example?"

Noor giggled. "No, thanks." She paused awkwardly. "Well, you were going somewhere, weren't you?"

"Yeah." Masoud lingered, but he suddenly felt a bit awkward himself. He said, "Well—uh—maybe we can talk when I get back."

"Sure," agreed Noor.

"Well, bye."

"*Ma'salama," said Noor.

"Yeah, ma'salama."

Noor felt really disappointed. "Maybe this isn't such a good test after all," she said to Whisper. "I think he's terrific! It doesn't really matter whether he likes my stupid poem or not."

"Stick with the plan," whispered the cat.

"Oh, now you want to help," she chastised Whisper.

The boys were gone most of the day. Noor spent her time memorizing Qur'an and sewing garments for poor children.

Finally in the afternoon, Noor heard Labeeb's voice rather loudly. "My coach slammed me onto the mat a hundred times today!" He was talking to his mother who was writing a note in the study. "I think that crazy coach is trying to kill me."

"If you're going to be in the army, you're getting the training you'll need," Amani said.

"I'd just prefer to die fighting for a *just cause* rather than die in *training*. That whacky martial arts instructor throws me around like I'm some kind of punching bag. I thought I wasn't going to survive today."

"Oh, it can't be that bad," Amani said as she sealed an envelope and left the room.

"Labeeb," Noor said shyly as she peeked into the room. "Would you like something to drink?"

"Oh, hi, Noor." Labeeb's voice suddenly turned soft and sweet. "Uh, yeah. I'll call for one of the servants to bring us something. I really got a workout today!"

"I'll get you something," Noor volunteered.

"No, you don't—," Labeeb started, but Noor was already running down the hall.

Noor returned with cold lemonade, salted nuts, olives, and deviled quail's eggs.

"Oh, you're a life saver, Noor," Labeeb said as Noor set the platter on a writing table in the study. "Thanks."

"Could I get your opinion on something?" Noor asked.

Labeeb nodded, grabbed a couple chairs, and arranged the chairs to face each other near the table.

"I thought this poem was really interesting, but I'm not sure what it means," Noor said as they both sat down. "Could you read it and tell me what you think?"

Labeeb took the paper, and Noor was pleased that he took time to carefully read the poem. Labeeb seemed to ponder every word. 'That's a good sign,' thought Noor.

"What it means to me, Noor," Labeeb said thoughtfully, "is that we need rules by which to live. If we don't have a society of ethics, values, and morals, then we are enslaved to sin and corruption. We find true freedom of spirit when our evil inclination is tethered by the rules of a just and moral society."

Noor was thrilled. "That's exactly what it—uh—I mean—that's what I think it means too. I guess we think alike. Isn't that great!" Noor looked away when she suddenly realized that she had gotten all bubbly with excitement.

"Yes, Noor; I think we have a lot in common."

Noor looked back at Labeeb and realized how much she truly loved his face—especially that slightly lopsided smile. She silently asked herself, 'Am I gazing flirtatiously?' and then she looked down.[26]

"You don't have to be shy with me, Noor," Labeeb said. "I'm not going to judge you."

'Oh, wow; he reads my mind too,' Noor thought.

Labeeb smiled, then leaned over and pinched her cheek. Noor felt giddy. Her heart seemed to have turned into butterflies. She grabbed the seat of her chair and held on with both hands to keep herself from pouncing on Labeeb and telling him how much she wanted to marry him. Somehow she managed to maintain what was left of her composure.

That night Noor fell asleep looking at the constellation Draco. She dreamed that she and Labeeb climbed onto the back of that magical dragon of stars. They flew throughout the universe as they sprinkled stardust on the world below. Her dreams were so wonderful that she didn't want to wake up. Too soon came the *adhan.

After the mid-day worship at the mosque, Noor returned to her room for writing materials. Whisper reminded, "Today's Hamsa's turn."

"What's the point?" Noor said. "Labeeb gave the perfect answer, the correct answer to the poem's meaning, and I think I'm in love now."

"Stick to the plan," whispered the sly, little cat.

"I guess it's only fair," said Noor. "I'm feeling guilty though. I don't want to hurt any of the boys' feelings. I'm still finding it difficult to believe that any one of them would want to marry the plain and strange Noor. To think that all three want me—well,

---

[26]Muslim men and women are taught not to cast flirtatious gazes (Surah 24: 30-31).

it's just hard to
believe. I hope the other two
won't be too hurt."

"They'll survive," promised Whisper, "and they'll find their own happiness."

Noor bounded downstairs. "I'm going to get a book on—I don't know—something about the military," she said to Whisper. "I heard Labeeb and Amani talking about Labeeb's joining the army. I should learn something about it so that I can support and encourage him in his career."

Noor was surprised to see Hamsa sitting at one of the library tables. He was engrossed in some old books.

"*Saba' al'kheer, Hamsa," Noor greeted.

"*Saba' anoor, and morning is light wherever Noor shines."

Noor blushed. She walked over and sat at the table with Hamsa. "What are you reading?"

"I'm studying *Sharia and how various interpretations of Qur'an have affected certain laws," he answered. "Can I help you find something?"

"Oh, no, I just came in here to sit and think." 'Why did I lie to him?' Noor silently chastised herself.

"I do that myself," Hamsa said. "When I have a problem to figure out, sometimes I just sit here surrounded by books. I like the way they look all orderly and united on the shelves. They're like a nation made up of different people who contribute their unique qualities to society. Every person is one part of the whole —like the Qur'an says. And we all need each other. Every person, like every good book, is valuable."

Hamsa was talking so softly that Noor had to lean close to hear him. She found herself drawn to him.

"Sometimes I feel like the books speak to me—I don't mean the words on the pages, but the books themselves," Hamsa continued. "Does that sound weird?"

"No," Noor quickly responded.

Hamsa smiled and continued. "They have so much knowledge to share. I like the way a book feels in my hand—like a familiar friend. I like the way the books smell— even the musty ones—*especially* the musty ones. They seem wiser, like sages on the mountain tops."

Noor thought that Hamsa was reading the words of her soul. She had always felt such things in the secret parts of her inner being, but she had never expressed them— even to herself. She thought how engaging Hamsa's eyes were—how they seemed to be worlds waiting to be explored. She suddenly realized that she was gazing at him as if in a daze. She looked away and straightened herself in the chair.

She thought of her poem, but now it seemed foolish and silly. Hamsa's words were so eloquent, so graceful; her stupid, little poem would probably be an insult to his intelligence. But Whisper jumped on the table and diligently stared at her; Noor knew exactly why, so she pulled the poem from her pocket.

Hamsa watched quietly as Noor slowly unfolded the paper.

"I have this poem. It's not very good. Maybe you could tell me what you think of it," said Noor.

"Did *you* write it?" Hamsa asked.

"Mmmhuh," Noor admitted, feeling embarrassed.

Hamsa read the poem slowly and smiled. "It's about me," he said.

'What!' Noor was baffled. How could he possibly be so vain as to think the poem was about him? "How do you mean?" she asked in a tone that hinted irritation.

"If my freedom meant living without you, my sweet, beautiful Noor, my spirit could never fly very high. By being chained by your love, I can escape the harshness of my own self interests." A tear settled in the corner of his eye. Embarrassed, Hamsa looked away.

'That was the wrong answer,' thought Noor. 'It was completely wrong. But it was *wonderfully* wrong.' At that moment, Noor wanted so much to embrace him.

"Umm, I need to go," Noor said as she rose from her chair.

Hamsa respectfully stood up too. "I have made a fool of myself, haven't I?" he said.

"No," Noor said almost breathlessly. "Oh, no. What you said was beautiful. It was just so beautiful, that I—I don't know what to say. Umm—I'll talk to you later; okay?"

"I *hope* we'll still be on speaking terms later," Hamsa joked with the same serious look with which his father joked. Noor was used to that, and it pleased her.

Noor ran up to her room. She shut the door behind her. "Aaaaaagh," she said out loud. "I want to marry *all* of them, Whisper! I hate being so lucky."

Noor stayed in her room all day. She needed time alone to think and pray. She thought, 'I want to make the right choice the first time and the only time. Even though Allah, *subhana wa ta'ala, permits divorce, Prophet Muhammed, *salAllahu alahe wa salam, said, *Of all the things that Allah allows, divorce is the most hateful.*'[27]

She thought of Masoud and how much fun he was to be around. He always had something clever to say. He knew how to make animal noises, and he could twist his

---

[27]A hadith reported by Abu Dawud.

face into all kinds of funny looks. 'But marriage isn't about entertainment,' thought Noor. 'I can't expect a husband to make me laugh all the time.'

She thought about Labeeb. He was so strong and dependable and handsome. He made her feel safe. 'But I have my own strength and independence,' thought Noor. 'And good looks fade.'

The feeling she experienced with Hamsa was different. She and Hamsa shared a comforting, gentle, easy kind of love —the kind of love she had seen modeled by Sultan Nabeeh and Sultana Amani. Hamsa's kind of thinking matched Noor's creative spirit. She had never known anyone like that before. He noticed her little quirks and liked them. He made her feel special—like—well, like royalty!

Losing at love is always painful. You can tell yourself that God has a better plan for you, but it still hurts. Masoud and Labeeb had their feelings hurt, but they found their own happiness. Masoud went to medical school and became a children's doctor who took time to make every patient feel special. He married a medical research doctor. Masoud and his wife worked together to build a complete medical center. It was the best anyone had ever seen. It was designed to meet all the needs of every patient. Labeeb finally beat his martial arts instructor (or did she *let* him win?). He realized that he was truly in love with her. He joined the army, but married his coach during his first leave. He encouraged his wife to enlist in the army. She served as a hand-to-hand combat instructor. Labeeb became a highly decorated soldier and a respected commanding officer.

Sultan Nabeeh and Sultana Amani were delighted that they had gained three daughters. They were glad that the kingdom would be left to two people with wisdom and capability. Hamsa and Noor began to learn the roles that, *insh'Allah, they would someday have. The Sultan and Sultana tried many of Hamsa's and Noor's creative ideas. The new ideas brought modern changes in government and society. A new age of useful thinking began, and people were able to plan for a bright future. The Kingdom of Sultan Nabeeh became a model of Islamic unity and goodness. It became a nation where every person was considered a unique blessing. All people were treated fairly and had equal opportunities. Everyone was free to become whatever God intended him or her to be. The Kingdom of Sultan Nabeeh became a nation where God was honored in every aspect of the great adventure called <u>LIFE</u>!

If you tried to count God's blessings,
you would not have enough numbers.
inspired by Surah 16:18

If you tried to list His wonders,
there would not be enough space.
If you tried to tell of them in a story,
there would not be enough words.
inspired by Psalms ✡ 40:6 († 40:5)

If all the trees on the earth were pens,
and all the oceans, plus seven more,
were ink, they would not be enough
to write the Knowledge of God.
inspired by Surah 31:27

GLOSSARY

abooya (a-boo-ya) <u>My father</u>. (Arabic)

adhan (ad-han) The Muslim call to prayer. (Arabic)

Afrah (af-ra) A female name meaning <u>happiness</u>. (Arabic)

Akbar (ak-bar) A male name meaning <u>great</u>. (Arabic)

alabaster (al-a-bas-ter) A translucent gypsum. Thin sheets were once used for windows.

alfalfa (al-fal-fa) A clover-like plant with purple flowers.

Al Fatiha (al fa-tee-a) <u>The Beginning</u>, the name of the first chapter of the Qur'an. (Arabic)

alhamdulAllah (al-ham-dul-la-la) <u>Praise God</u>. (Arabic)

Ali (a-lee) A male name meaning <u>excellence</u>. (Arabic)

Allah (al-la) The One True God, the God of Adam and Eve, Noah, Mary, Jesus, and Muhammed, and all the other prophets of God. (English from Arabic)

Allahu akbar (al-la-hoo ak-bar) <u>God is great</u>. (Arabic)

alleluyah (al-la-loo-ya) <u>Praise God</u>. (Hebrew)

amal (a-mal) <u>Hope</u>. (Arabic)

Amani (a-ma-nee) A female name meaning <u>aspirations</u>. (Arabic)

Ameera (a-meer-a) A female name meaning <u>princess</u>. (Arabic)

amputation (am-pu-ta-shun) The surgical removal of a limb.

Asah (a-sa) A female name taken from the name of a Middle Eastern plant. (Arabic)

asalam alaiekum (a-sa-lam a-la-ee-kum) <u>Peace be upon you</u>, the universal Muslim greeting. (Arabic)

Azhar (az-har) A female name meaning <u>flower blossoms</u>. (Arabic)

Banat al Lah (ba-nat al la) <u>Daughters of God</u>, the pagan goddesses al Lat, al Uzza, and Manat. (Arabic)

Bedouin (bed-oo-in) An Arab of any of the nomadic tribes of the deserts of North Africa, Arabia, and Syria (English from Arabic)

BismAllah (bis-mal-la) <u>In the name of God</u>. (Arabic)

brocade (bro-kaad) A fabric with a raised, interwoven design.

Buddhist (boo-dist) A person who follows the teachings of Buddha, a prince of India who gave up his throne in search of wisdom and enlightenment (Buddhists do not believe in One God, but they believe in the spiritual realm and that the spirit of every particle of creation is equally important.)

Bushra (bush-ra) A female name indicating a good omen. (Arabic)

cannibalism (kan-a-ba-liz-em) A human's eating the flesh of another human.

circumnavigation (sur-kum-nav-i-ga-shun) The act of sailing around.

couscous (coos-coos) A Middle Eastern pasta made of semolina and having a consistency coarser than cream of wheat and finer than grits.

disheveled (di-shev-eled) Past tense of *dishevel*, to disarrange the hair and/or clothing of a person.

du'a (doo-ah) Personal prayer. (Arabic)

El Shaddai (el shad-di) <u>God Almighty</u>. (Hebrew)

entourage (an-too-razh) A long line of attendants.

frugal (froo-gal) Avoiding unnecessary spending.

garnisheed (gar-nished) Past tense of *garnishee*, to deduct a debt from wages (pronounced the same as *garnish*, to embellish).

geode (jee-od) A round, gray or brown, hollow rock with crystals lining the inside wall.

Hamsa (ham-sa) Also spelled *Hamza*. A male name meaning <u>lion</u>. (Arabic)

Hadith (ha-deeth) The collected teachings of Muhammed. (Arabic)

Iblis (ib-lis) Satan's name given in the Qur'an. (Arabic)

ibn (ib-en) <u>Son of</u>. (Arabic)

ibnee (ib-nee) <u>My son</u>. (Arabic)

Ibrahim (ee-bra-heem) A name corresponding to the English <u>Abraham</u>. (Arabic)

Ilham (il-ham) A female name meaning <u>inspiration</u>. (Arabic)

indelible (in-del-e-bel) Permanent, non-fading.

insh'Allah (in-sha-al-la) <u>If God is willing</u>. (Arabic)

imam (e-mam) Muslim prayer leader. (Arabic)

Islam (i-slam) 1. Complete submission to God, the faith believed by Muslims to be the original religion ordained by God to Adam and Eve and all creation. 2. The organized religion based on the Qur'an and the Sunnah (examples) and aHadeeth (teachings) of Muhammed. 3. The term used by Muslims to describe the peace a believer feels when he or she submits his or her whole self to God. (English from Arabic)

jade (jad) 1. A light to medium green mineral used as a gemstone. 2. The color of jade.

Jameela (ja-meel-a) A female name meaning <u>beautiful</u>. (Arabic)

jini (gin-ee) plural: *jinn* 1. In pre-Islam: a kind, mischievous, or evil spirit, based on superstition, able to appear in various forms. 2. In the Qur'an: an angelic being who exercises free will, some for good, some for evil. (Arabic)

Ka'bah (ka-ba) The House of God believed to be built by Abraham and Ishmael in Meccah, Saudi Arabia. (Arabic)

keef halak? (keef hal-ak) <u>How are you</u>? to a man (*keef halik?* to a woman). (Arabic)

kufi (koo-fee) Muslim man's prayer cap. (Arabic)

kutba (koot-ba) <u>Sermon</u>. (Arabic)

Labeeb (la-beeb) A male name meaning <u>sensible</u>. (Arabic)

La illaha illa Allah; Muhammedan rasulAllah (la il-la-ha il-la al-la; mu-ham-med-an ra-sool-al-la) The Muslim confession of faith (called *shahada*): <u>There is no god but God; Muhammed is the messenger of God</u>. (Arabic)

Maisa (mi-ee-sa) A female name which indicates walking with pride. (Arabic)

masjid (mas-jid) <u>Mosque</u>, the Muslim house of prayer and worship. (Arabic)

marhaba (mar-ha-ba) <u>Hello</u>. (Arabic)

Maryam (ma-ree-om) A name corresponding to the English <u>Mary</u> and the Hebrew <u>Miriam</u>. (Arabic)

Masoud (ma-sood) A male name meaning <u>happy-go-lucky</u>. (Arabic)

ma'salama (ma-sa-la-ma) <u>With peace</u> (used in bidding farewell). (Arabic)

minaret (men-e-ret) A tall, slender tower on a mosque.

mirage (mi-razh) An optical illusion, often on sand or snow and sometimes created by reflections of distant objects.

mitzvot (mits-vot) plural of *mitzvah*. Often translated to *good deeds*, but to the Jew an act of mitzvah means much more because the act is a testament to the vitality of the covenant into which Jews have entered with God.

mufassir (moo-fas-seer) plural: *mufassireen*. A person who interprets the meanings of the Qur'an. (Arabic)

Muslim (muz-lim) Also spelled *Moslem*. 1. One who submits his or her whole self to God. 2. One who chooses to follow the Islamic faith. 3. One who is born into the Muslim community and is considered Muslim by heritage. (Such a person, however, must eventually make his or her own choice whether or not to accept Islam into his or her heart.) (English from Arabic)

muzien (moo-zeen) The person giving the Muslim call to prayer. (Arabic)

Nabeeh (na-bee) A male name meaning <u>noble</u>. (Arabic)

Noor (noor) A female name meaning <u>light</u>. (Arabic)

nun (nun) A religious woman (Catholic or Episcopalian) who has taken a vow of chastity and devoted her life to God.

precedent (pres-a-dent) An action that can be used as an example in similar situations.

Qur'an (koor-an) Also spelled *Koran*. The <u>Revelation</u> delivered by the angel Gabriel to Prophet Muhammed. (English from Arabic)

rabbi (rab-i) 1. <u>Teacher</u>. 2. The ordained spiritual leader of a Jewish congregation. Capitalized when referring to a specific rabbi. (English from Hebrew)

ramatullah (ra-ma-tul-la) <u>God bless you</u>. (Arabic)

Raatib (ra-teeb) A male name meaning <u>one who arranges things</u>. (Arabic)

rabies (ra-beez) A serious and usually fatal viral disease attacking the central nervous system of some mammals. The virus drives the animal (or person) mad with symptoms of hydrophobia (fear of water) and violent rage. It is contagious and is transferred by infectious bites.

renegade (ren-a-gaad) Outlaw.

Riyad (ree-yad) A male name meaning <u>gardens</u>. (Arabic)

saba' al'kheer (sa-ba al-kheer) <u>Morning of goodness</u>; used as "good morning." (Arabic)

saba' anoor (sa-ba a-noor) <u>Morning of light</u>; used as "good morning." (Arabic)

sage (saj) A wise and spiritual person worthy of respect.

salAllahu alahe wa salam (sa-lal-la-hoo a-la-he wa sa-lam) <u>May the peace and blessings of God be upon him</u>, the blessing spoken or written after the name of Prophet Muhammed. (Arabic)

salat (sa-lat) The Muslim ritual of worship involving prayers, praises, and recitations. (Arabic)

salam (sa-lam) <u>Peace</u>. (Arabic)

Sariyah (sa-re-yah) A male name meaning <u>clouds at night</u>. (Arabic)

shalom (sha-lom) <u>Peace</u>. (Hebrew)

shalom alekhem (sha-lom a-le-kh'em) <u>Peace be upon you</u>. (Hebrew)

Sharia (sha-ree-a) Islamic law based on the Qur'an and the Hadith (teachings) and Sunnah (examples) of Prophet Muhammed. (Arabic)

sheik (sheek) The leader of an Arab tribe.

Souhail (soo-hal) The name of a star; a male name. (Arabic)

subhana wa ta'ala (soob-ha-na wa ta-a-la) <u>May He be glorified and exalted</u>, the statement of praise offered after the Name of God. (Arabic)

sultan (sul-tan) A Muslim king. Capitalized when referring to a specific sultan. (English from Arabic)

sultana (sul-tan-a) The mother, wife, sister, or daughter of a sultan. Capitalized when referring to a specific sultana. (English from Arabic)

Sunnah (soo-na) The examples of the Prophet Muhammed, which guide Muslims in how to live an exemplary life. (Arabic)

surah (soo-ra) <u>Chapter</u>, refers to a chapter of the Qur'an. (Arabic)

synagogue (sin-a-gog) Jewish house of prayer and worship.

tafaddalee (ta-fad-da-lee) <u>Please</u>, when extending an invitation to a female (to a male: *tafaddal*). (Arabic)

Tamam (ta-mam) A male name meaning <u>generous</u>. (Arabic)

ummah (oo-ma) 1. Religious congregation of an individual church, synagogue, or mosque. 2. The universal family of Muslims. 3. The universal family of all believers of the One True God. (Arabic; also Aramaic, the language of Jesus)

ummee (um-mee) <u>My mother</u>. (Arabic)

Usamah (o-sa-ma) A male name referring to the qualities of a lion. (Arabic)

usury (yoo-ze-ree) An excessive and unfair amount of interest added to a debt.

Wajeeh (wa-jee) A male name meaning <u>noble</u>. (Arabic)

Yasir (ya-sur) A male name meaning <u>wealthy</u>. (Arabic)

Yusuf (yoo-suf) The Arabic name corresponding to the English <u>Joseph</u>.